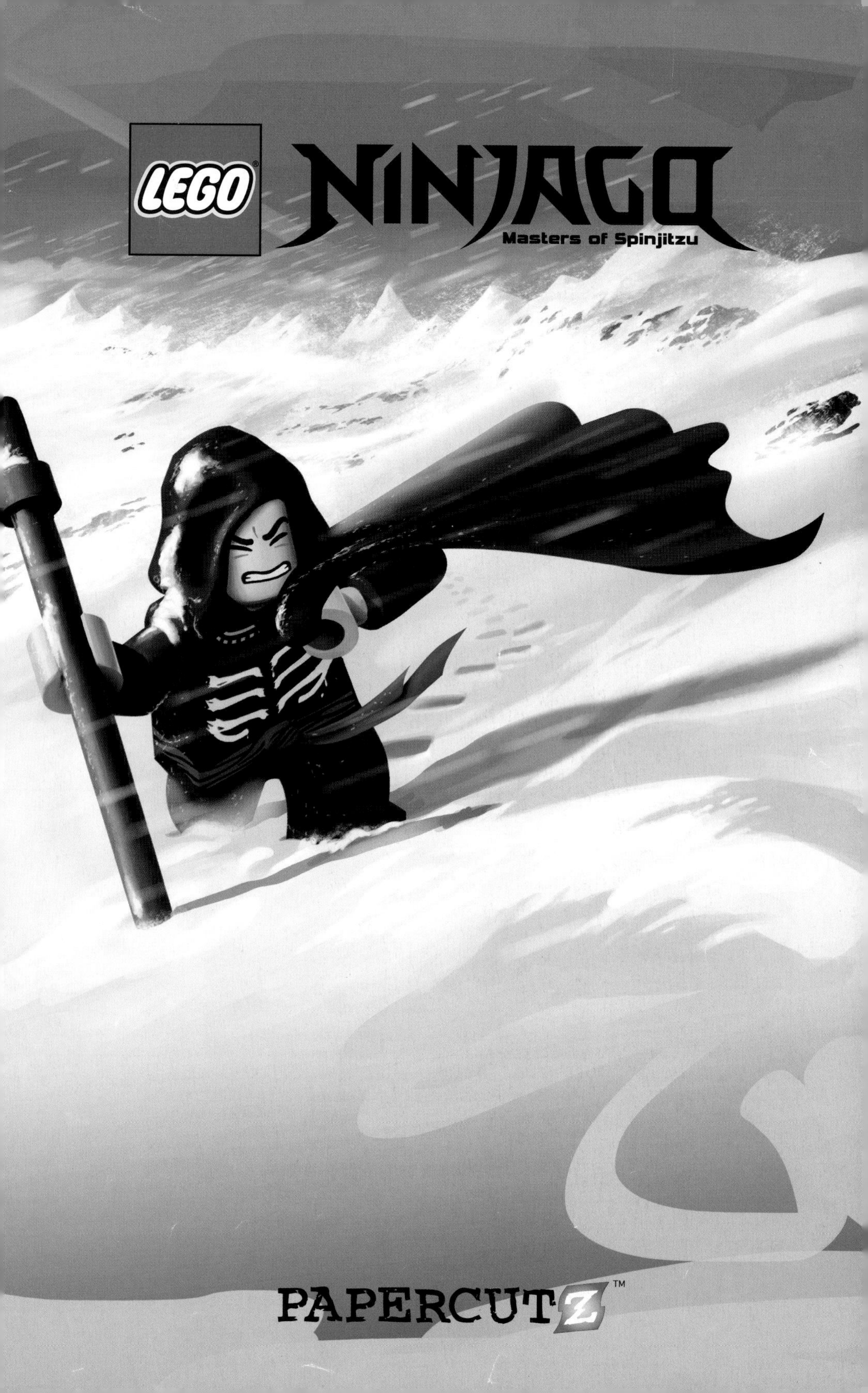
LEGO
NINJAGO
Masters of Spinjitzu
PAPERCUTZ

LEGO® GRAPHIC NOVELS AVAILABLE FROM PAPERCUTZ

ALL-NEW! FULL-COLOR GRAPHIC NOVEL!
LEGO NINJAGO
"THE CHALLENGE OF SAMUKAI"
GREG FARSHTEY
PAULO HENRIQUE
PAPERCUTZ

LEGO NINJAGO #1

ALL-NEW! FULL-COLOR GRAPHIC NOVEL!
LEGO NINJAGO
"MASK OF THE SENSEI"
PAPERCUTZ

LEGO NINJAGO #2

ALL-NEW! FULL-COLOR GRAPHIC NOVEL!
LEGO NINJAGO
"RISE OF THE SERPENTINE"
GREG FARSHTEY
PAUL LEE
PAPERCUTZ

LEGO NINJAGO #3

ALL-NEW! FULL-COLOR GRAPHIC NOVEL!
LEGO NINJAGO
"TOMB OF THE FANGPYRE"
GREG FARSHTEY
JOLYON YATES
PAPERCUTZ

LEGO NINJAGO #4

ALL-NEW! FULL-COLOR GRAPHIC NOVEL!
LEGO NINJAGO
"KINGDOM OF THE SNAKES"
GREG FARSHTEY
JOLYON YATES
PAPERCUTZ

LEGO NINJAGO #5

ALL-NEW! FULL-COLOR GRAPHIC NOVEL!
LEGO NINJAGO
"WARRIORS OF STONE"
GREG FARSHTEY
JOLYON YATES
PAPERCUTZ

LEGO NINJAGO #6

ALL-NEW! FULL-COLOR GRAPHIC NOVEL!
LEGO NINJAGO
STONE COLD
GREG FARSHTEY • JOLYON YATES
PAPERCUTZ

LEGO NINJAGO #7

ALL-NEW! FULL-COLOR GRAPHIC NOVEL!
LEGO NINJAGO
"DESTINY OF DOOM"
GREG FARSHTEY
JOLYON YATES
PAPERCUTZ

LEGO NINJAGO #8

COMING SOON!

LEGO NINJAGO #9

SPECIAL EDITION
LEGO NINJAGO
2 GRAPHIC NOVELS IN 1
IT ALL BEGINS HERE--
WITH "THE CHALLENGE OF SAMUKAI" AND "THE MASK OF THE SENSEI"
GREG FARSHTEY
PAULO HENRIQUE
PAPERCUTZ

SPECIAL EDITION #1
(Features stories from
NINJAGO #1 & #2.)

SPECIAL EDITION
LEGO NINJAGO
2 GRAPHIC NOVELS IN 1
"RISE OF THE SERPENTINE" AND "TOMB OF THE FANGPYRE"
GREG FARSHTEY
PAUL LEE
JOLYON YATES
PAPERCUTZ

SPECIAL EDITION #2
(Features stories from
NINJAGO #3 & #4.)

SPECIAL EDITION
LEGO NINJAGO
2 GRAPHIC NOVELS IN 1
"KINGDOM OF THE SNAKES" AND "WARRIORS OF STONE"
GREG FARSHTEY
JOLYON YATES
PAPERCUTZ

SPECIAL EDITION #3
(Features stories from
NINJAGO #5 & #6.)

LEGO® NINJAGO graphic novels are available in paperback and hardcover at booksellers everywhere.

You can also order online at papercutz.com. Or call 1-800-886-1223, Monday through Friday, 9 – 5 EST. MC, Visa, and AmEx accepted. To order by mail, please add $4.00 for postage and handling for first book ordered, $1.00 for each additional book and make check payable to NBM Publishing. Send to: Papercutz, 160 Broadway, Suite 700, East Wing, New York, NY 10038.

LEGO NINJAGO graphic novels are also available digitally wherever e-books are sold.

DESTINY OF DOOM

Greg Farshtey – Writer
Jolyon Yates – Artist
Laurie E. Smith – Colorist

PAPERCUTZ™
New York

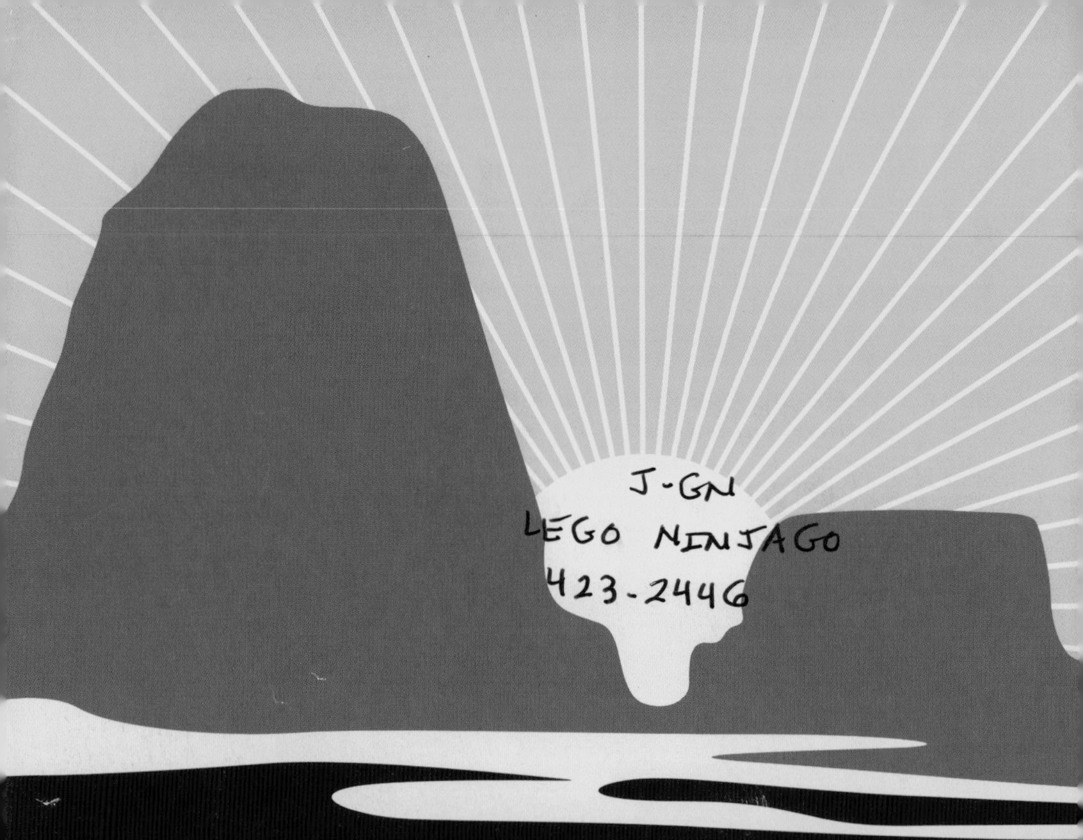

LEGO® NINJAGO Masters of Spinjitzu
#8 "Destiny of Doom"

GREG FARSHTEY – Writer
JOLYON YATES – Artist
LAURIE E. SMITH – Colorist
BRYAN SENKA – Letterer
DAWN K. GUZZO – Production
BETH SCORZATO – Production Coordinator
STAN LEE & JACK KIRBY – Special Thanks
MICHAEL PETRANEK – Associate Editor
JIM SALICRUP
Editor-in-Chief

ISBN: 978-1-59707-481-0 paperback edition
ISBN: 978-1-59707-480-3 hardcover edition

Papercutz books may be purchased for business or promotional use. For information on bulk purchases please contact Macmillan Corporate and Premium Sales Department at (800) 221-7945 x5442.

Printed in the USA
August 2013 by Lifetouch Printing
5126 Forest Hills Ct.
Loves Park, IL 61111

Distributed by Macmillan

First Printing

FSC
www.fsc.org
MIX
Paper from
responsible sources
FSC® C112431

MEET THE MASTERS OF SPINJITZU...

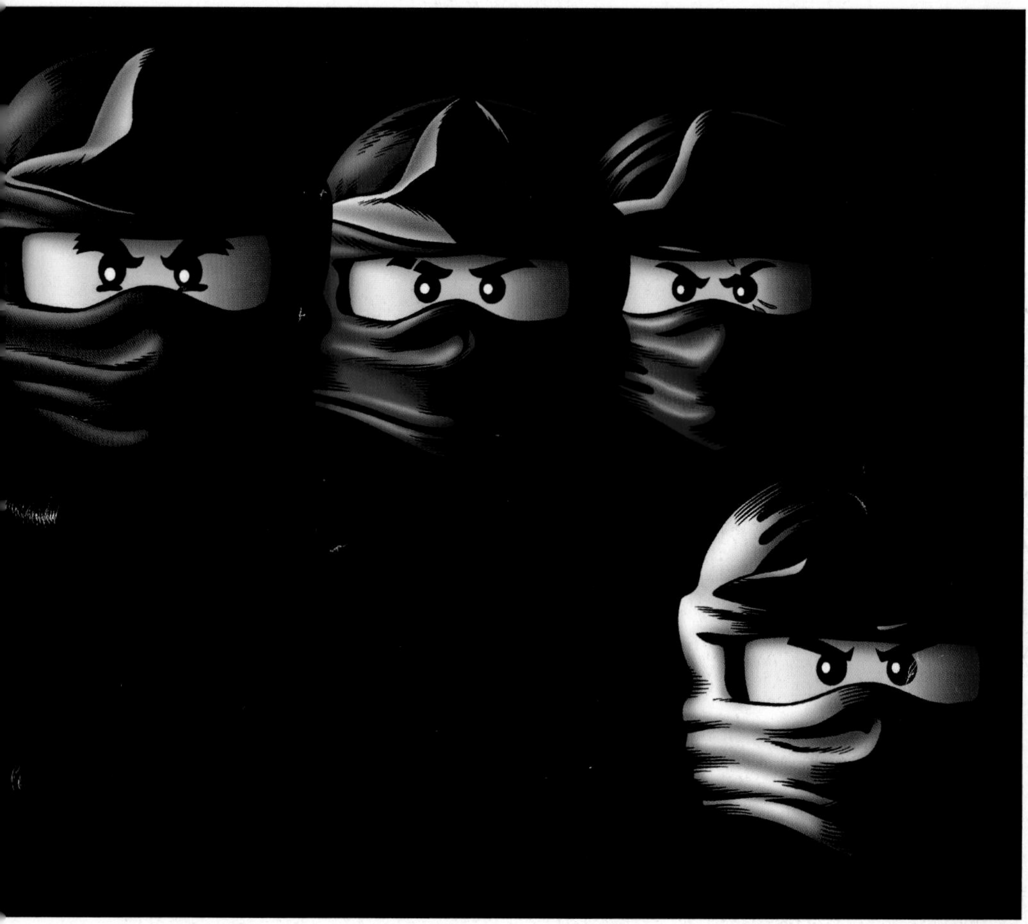

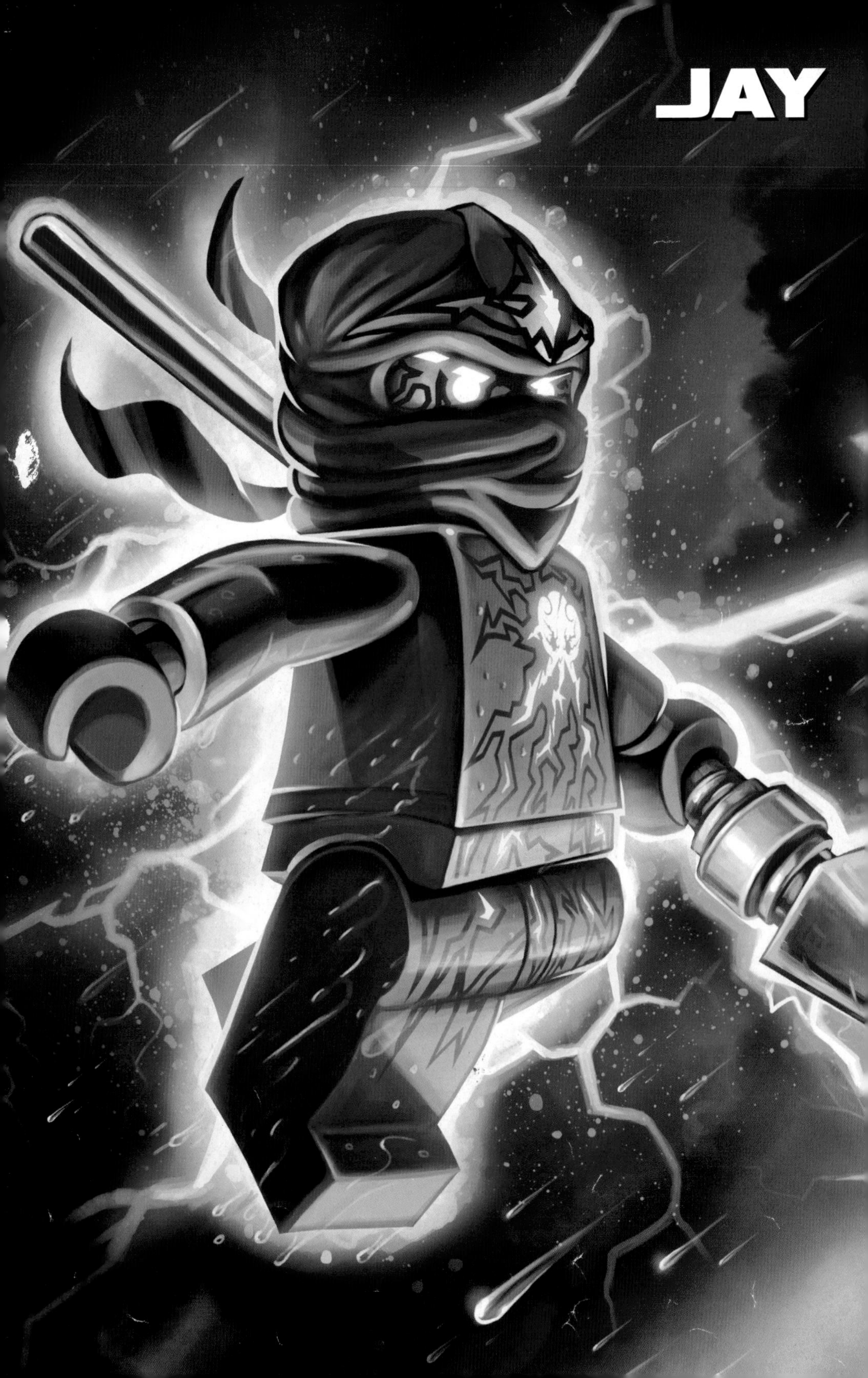
JAY

COLE

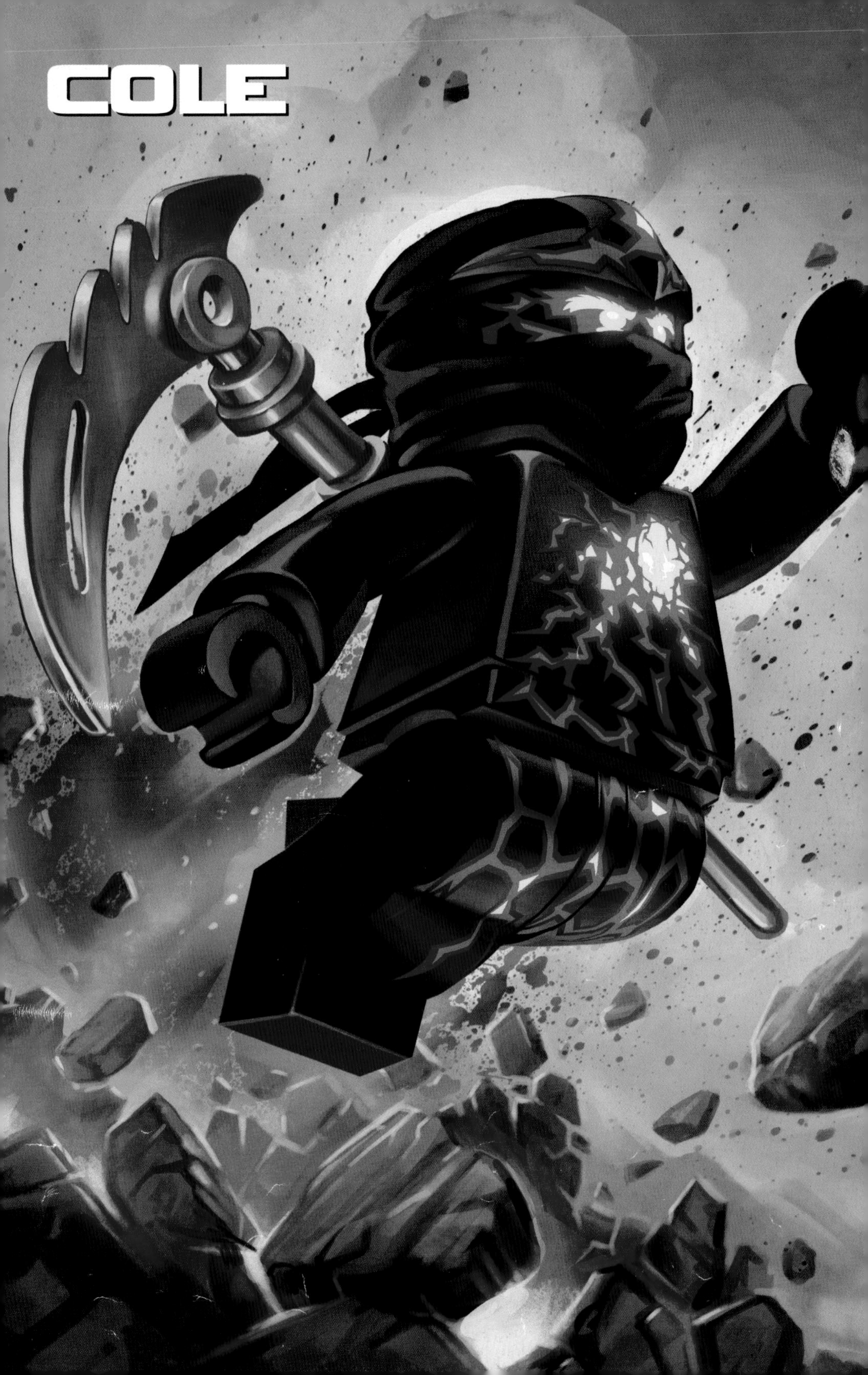

ZANE

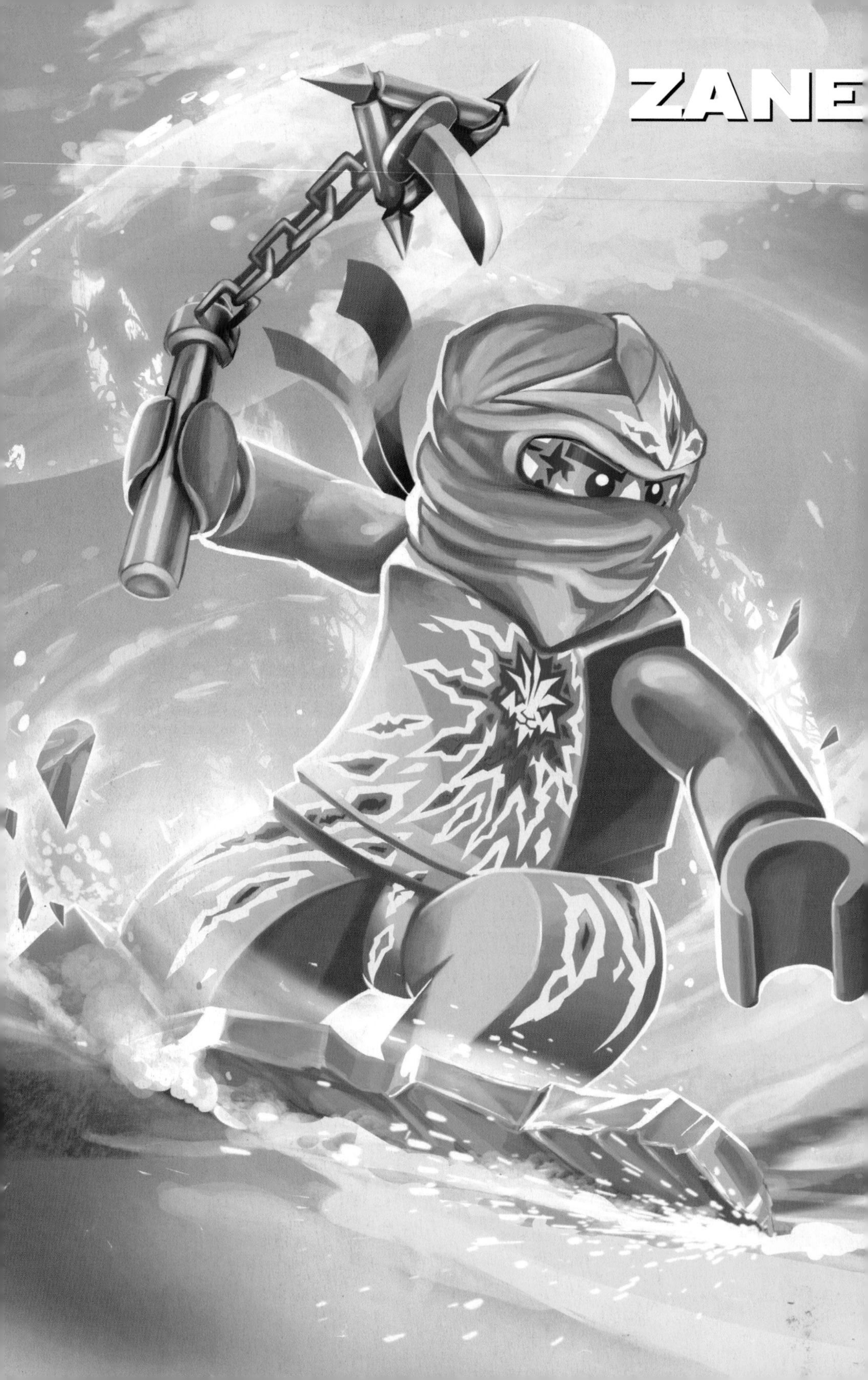

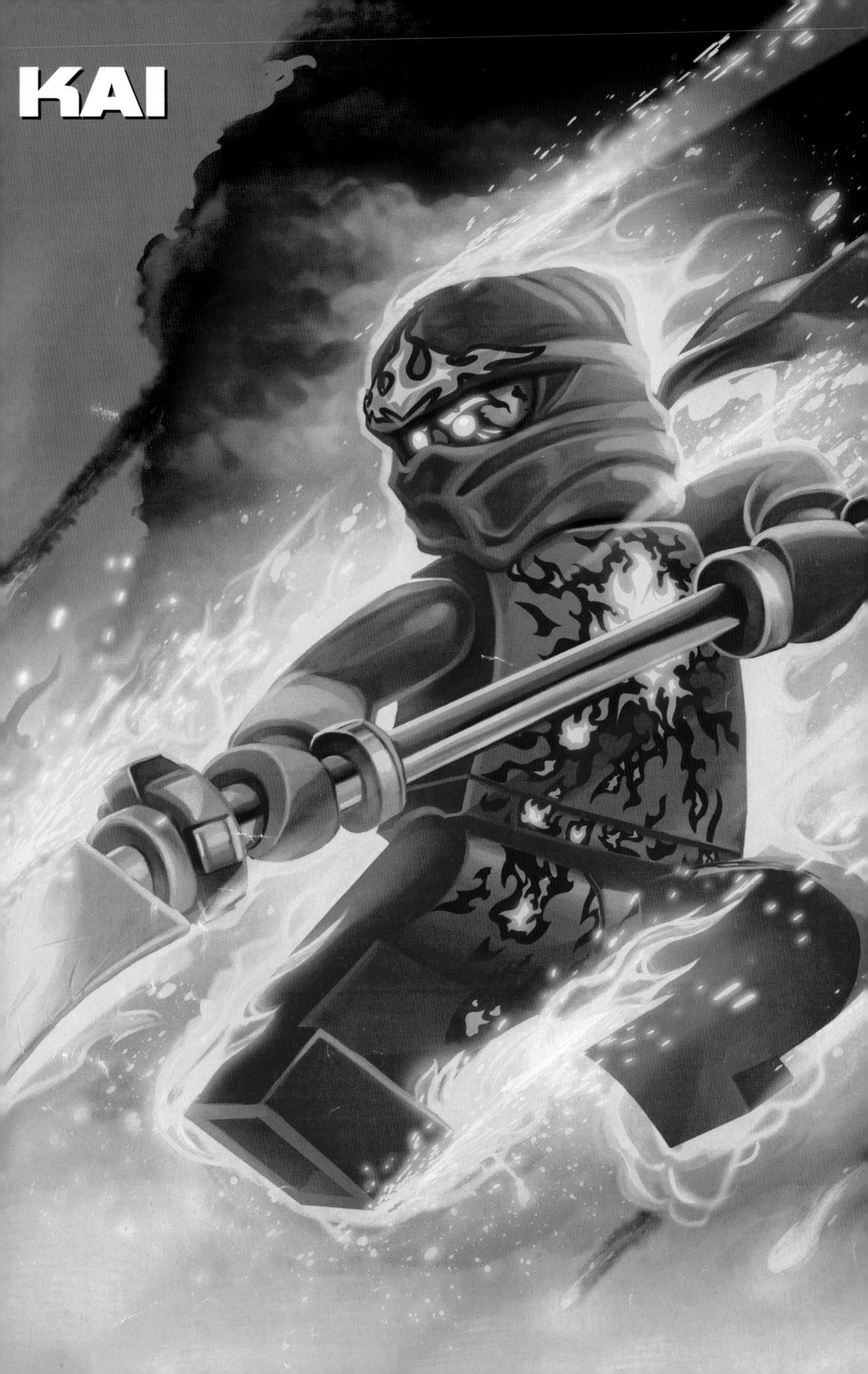
KAI

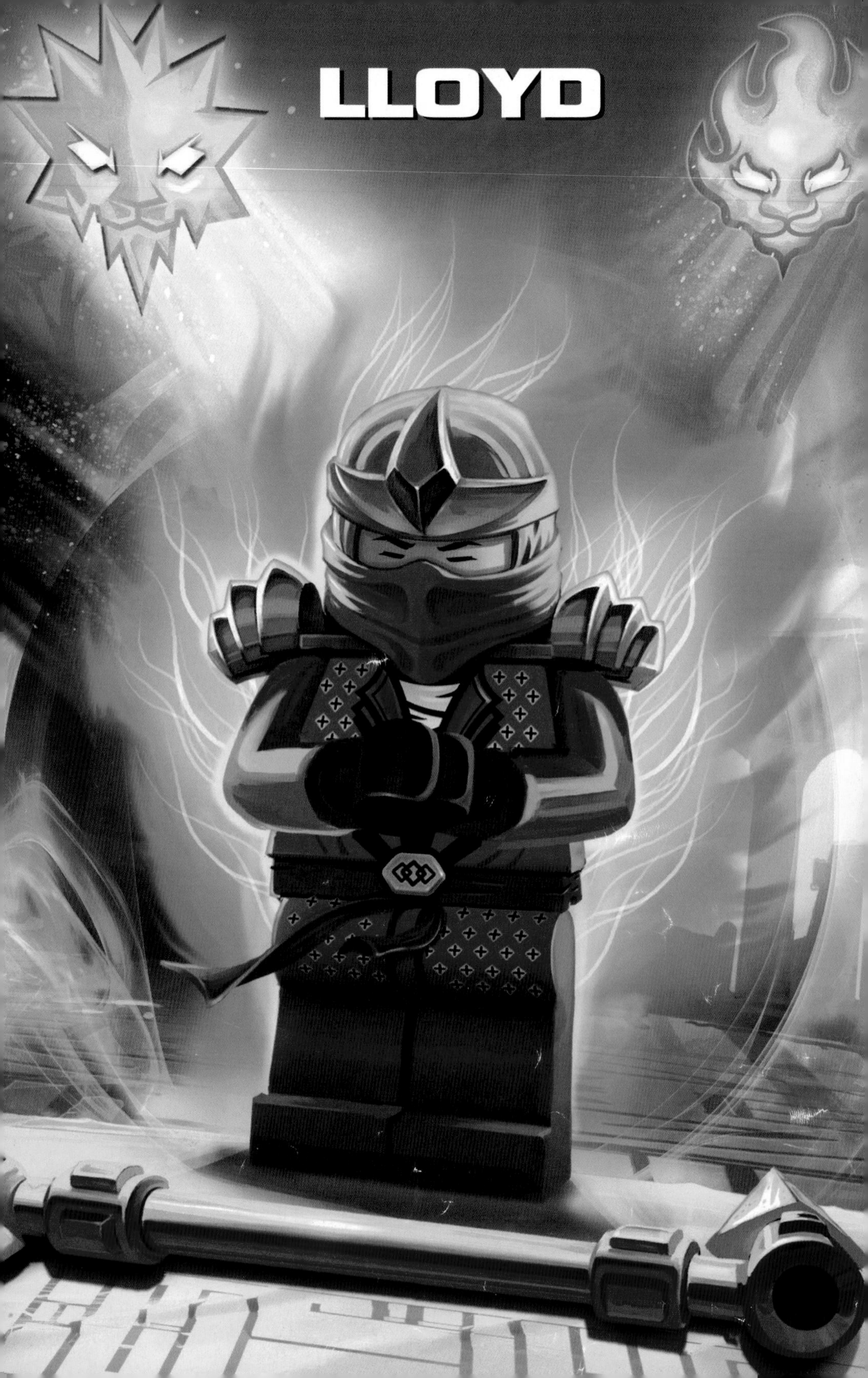
LLOYD

And the Master of the Masters of Spinjitzu...

SENSEI WU

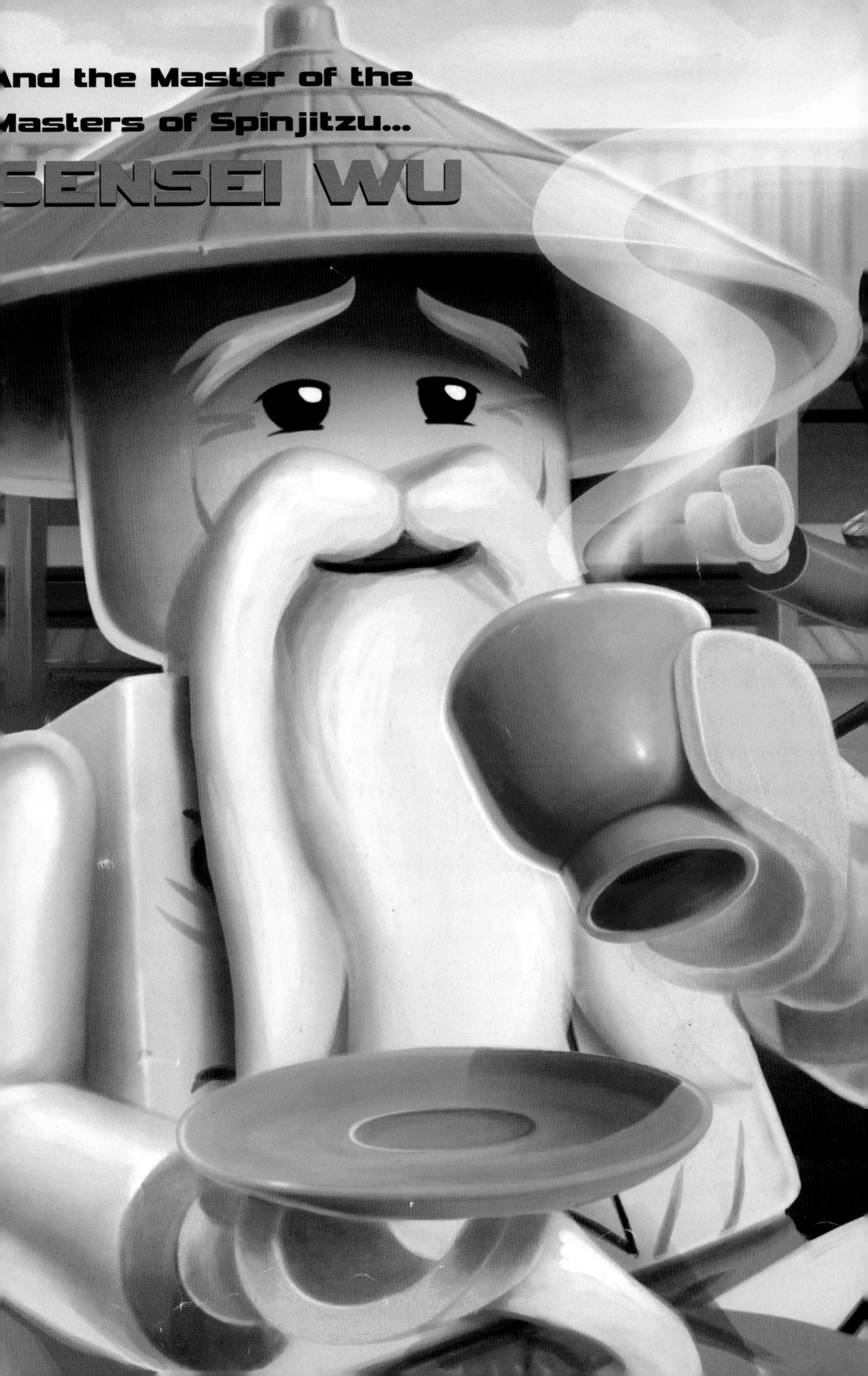

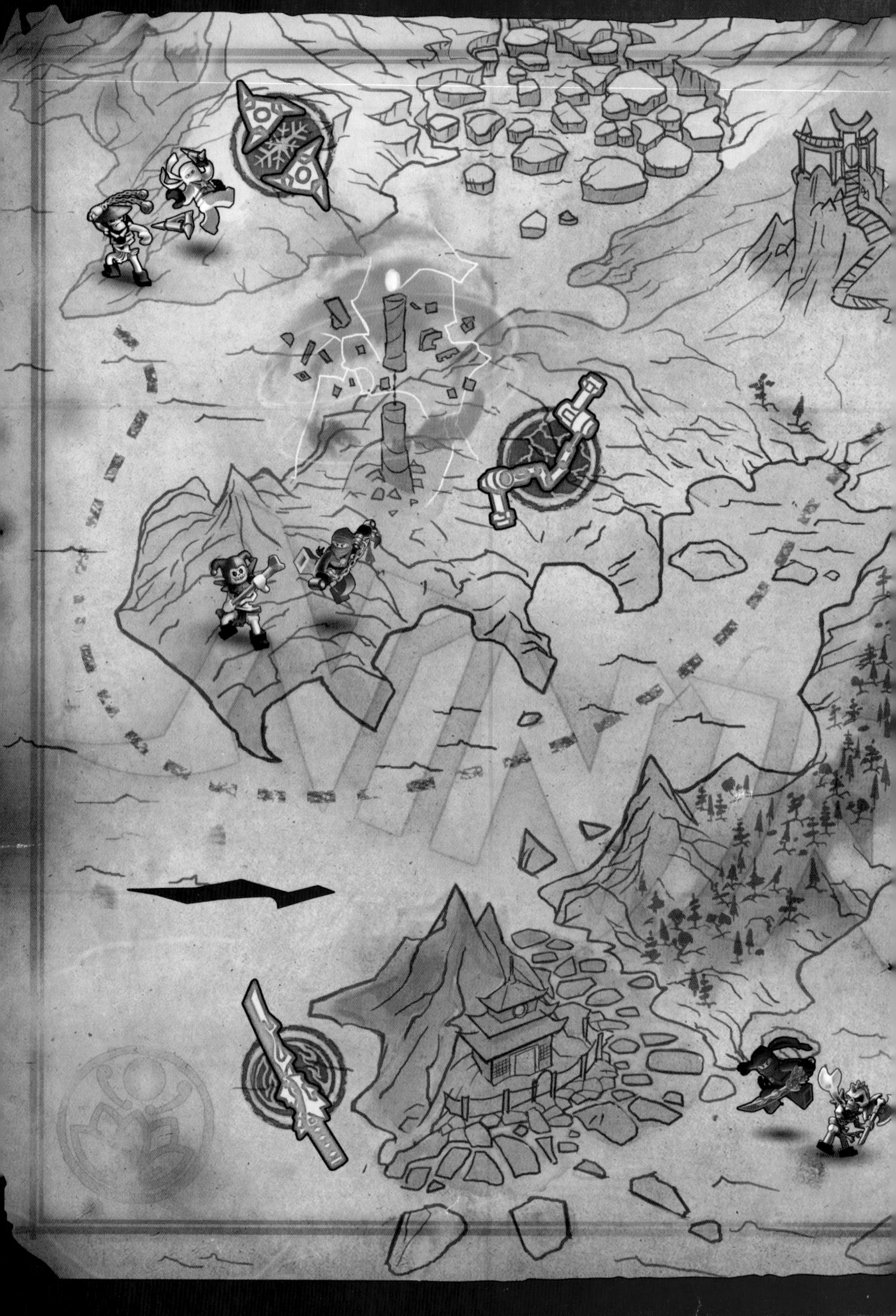

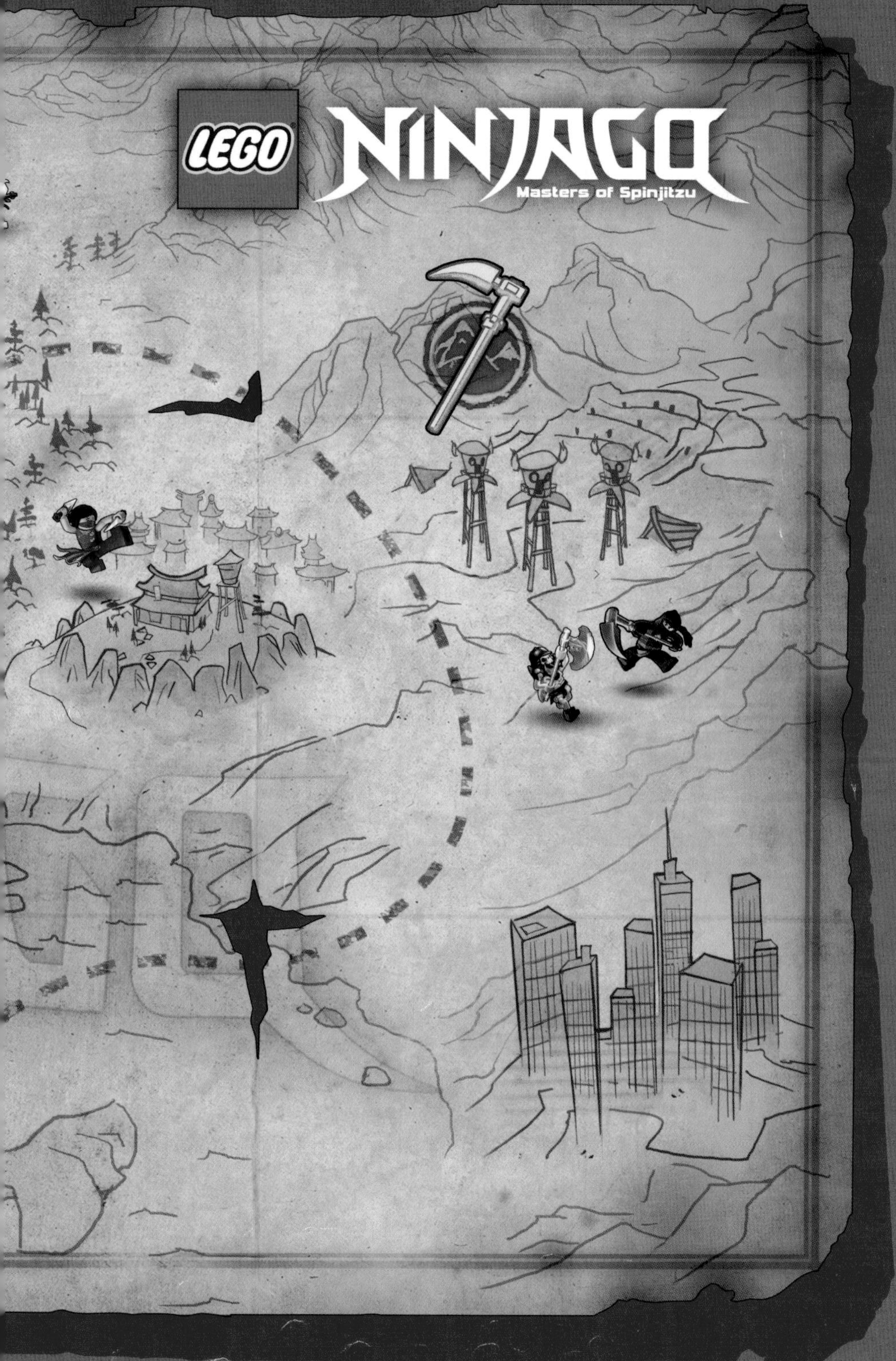
LEGO
NINJAGO
Masters of Spinjitzu

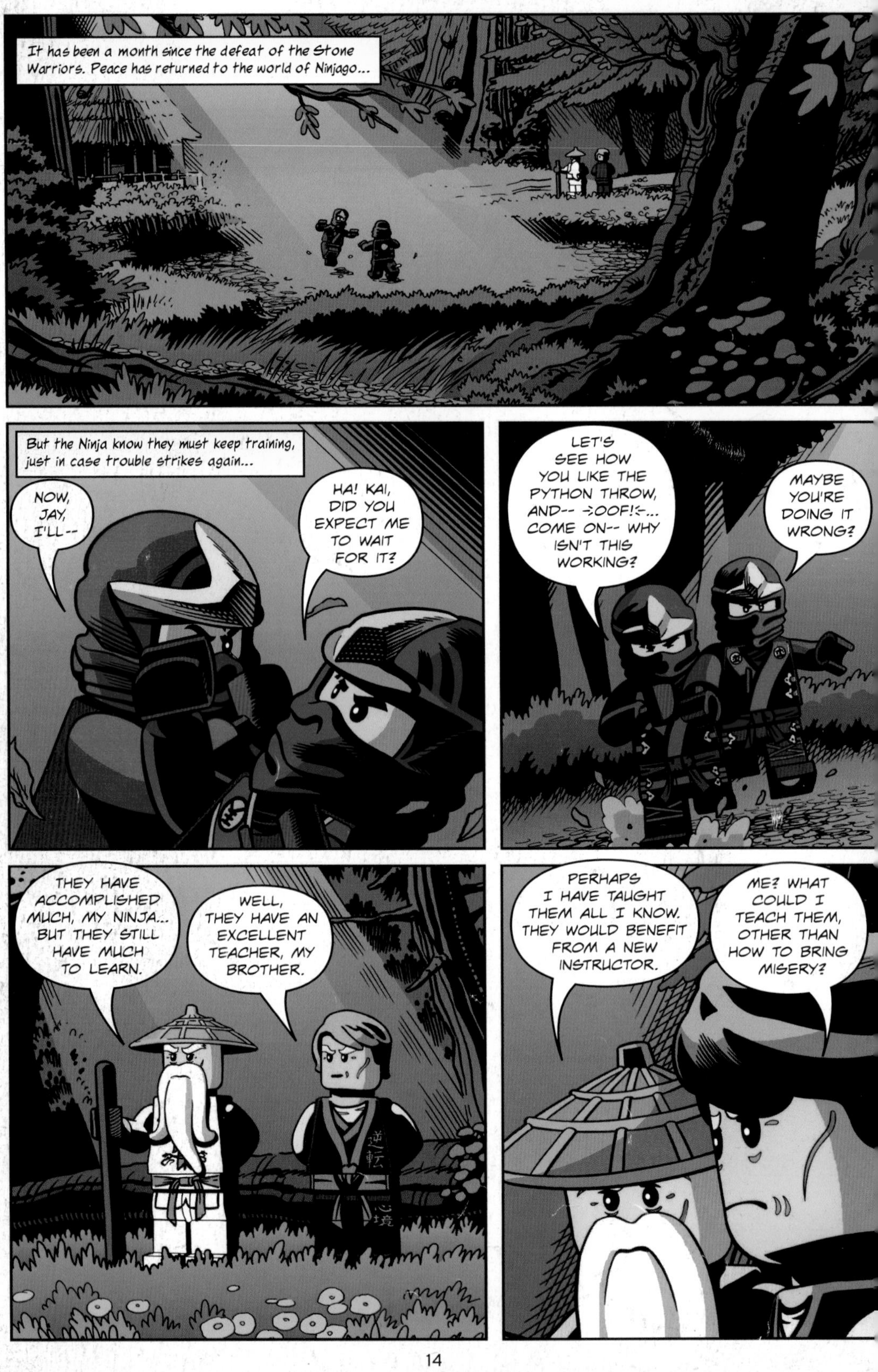

It has been a month since the defeat of the Stone Warriors. Peace has returned to the world of Ninjago...
But the Ninja know they must keep training, just in case trouble strikes again...
NOW, JAY, I'LL--
HA! KAI, DID YOU EXPECT ME TO WAIT FOR IT?
LET'S SEE HOW YOU LIKE THE PYTHON THROW, AND-- >OOF!<... COME ON-- WHY ISN'T THIS WORKING?
MAYBE YOU'RE DOING IT WRONG?
THEY HAVE ACCOMPLISHED MUCH, MY NINJA... BUT THEY STILL HAVE MUCH TO LEARN.
WELL, THEY HAVE AN EXCELLENT TEACHER, MY BROTHER.
PERHAPS I HAVE TAUGHT THEM ALL I KNOW. THEY WOULD BENEFIT FROM A NEW INSTRUCTOR.
ME? WHAT COULD I TEACH THEM, OTHER THAN HOW TO BRING MISERY?

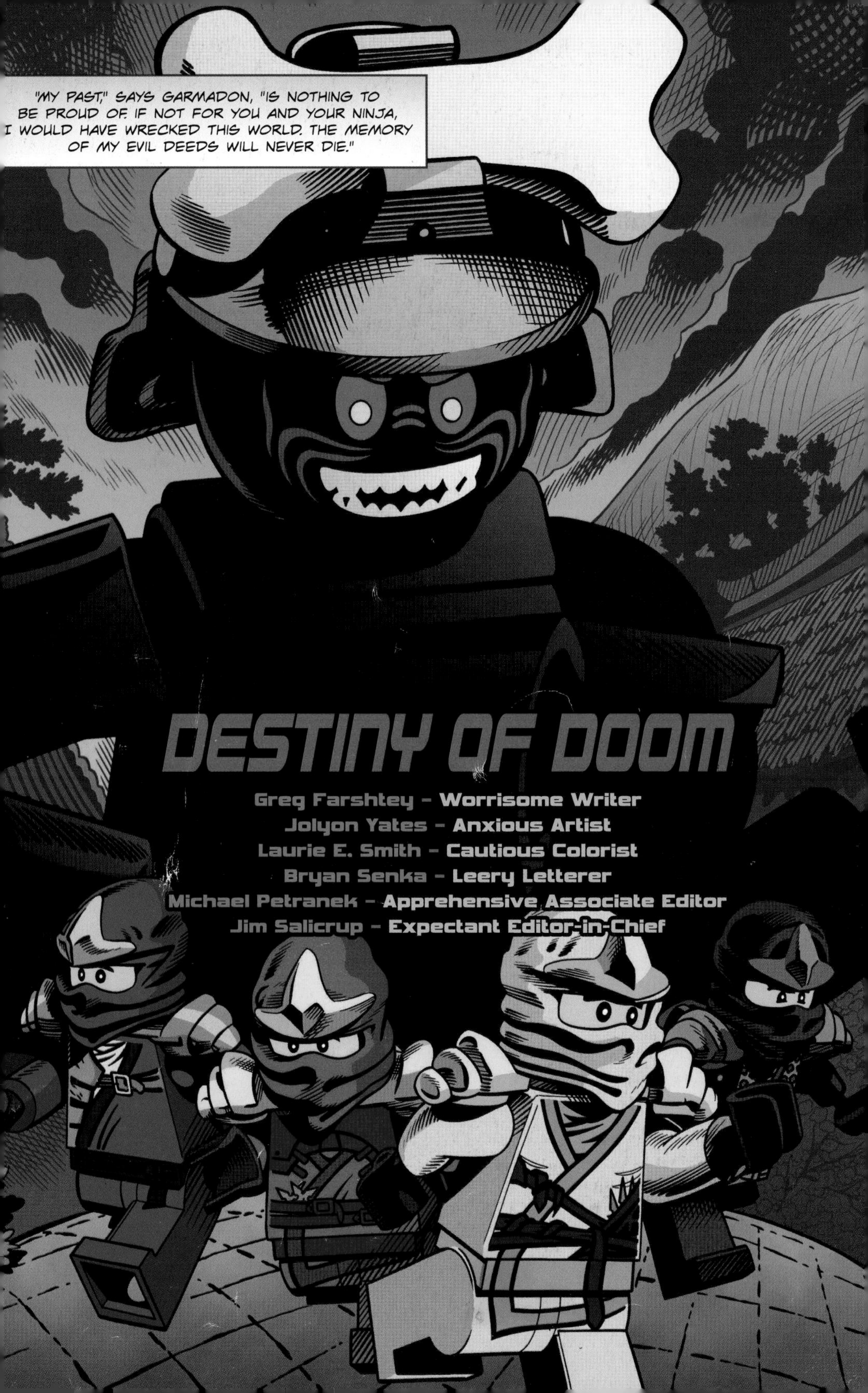
"MY PAST," SAYS GARMADON, "IS NOTHING TO BE PROUD OF. IF NOT FOR YOU AND YOUR NINJA, I WOULD HAVE WRECKED THIS WORLD. THE MEMORY OF MY EVIL DEEDS WILL NEVER DIE."
DESTINY OF DOOM
Greg Farshtey – Worrisome Writer
Jolyon Yates – Anxious Artist
Laurie E. Smith – Cautious Colorist
Bryan Senka – Leery Letterer
Michael Petranek – Apprehensive Associate Editor
Jim Salicrup – Expectant Editor-in-Chief

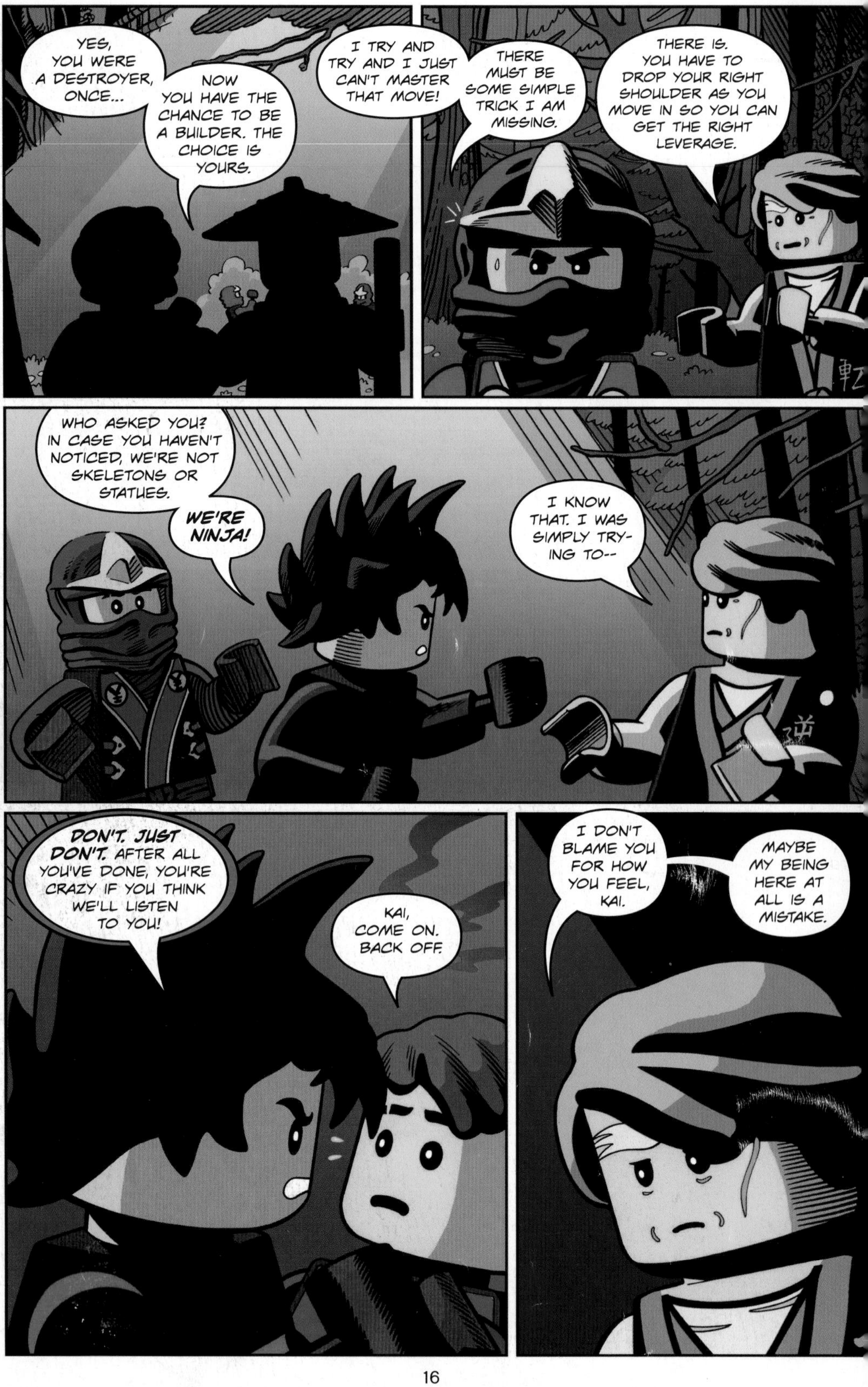
YES, YOU WERE A DESTROYER, ONCE...
NOW YOU HAVE THE CHANCE TO BE A BUILDER. THE CHOICE IS YOURS.
I TRY AND TRY AND I JUST CAN'T MASTER THAT MOVE!
THERE MUST BE SOME SIMPLE TRICK I AM MISSING.
THERE IS. YOU HAVE TO DROP YOUR RIGHT SHOULDER AS YOU MOVE IN SO YOU CAN GET THE RIGHT LEVERAGE.
WHO ASKED YOU? IN CASE YOU HAVEN'T NOTICED, WE'RE NOT SKELETONS OR STATUES.
WE'RE NINJA!
I KNOW THAT. I WAS SIMPLY TRY-ING TO--
DON'T. JUST DON'T. AFTER ALL YOU'VE DONE, YOU'RE CRAZY IF YOU THINK WE'LL LISTEN TO YOU!
KAI, COME ON. BACK OFF.
I DON'T BLAME YOU FOR HOW YOU FEEL, KAI.
MAYBE MY BEING HERE AT ALL IS A MISTAKE.

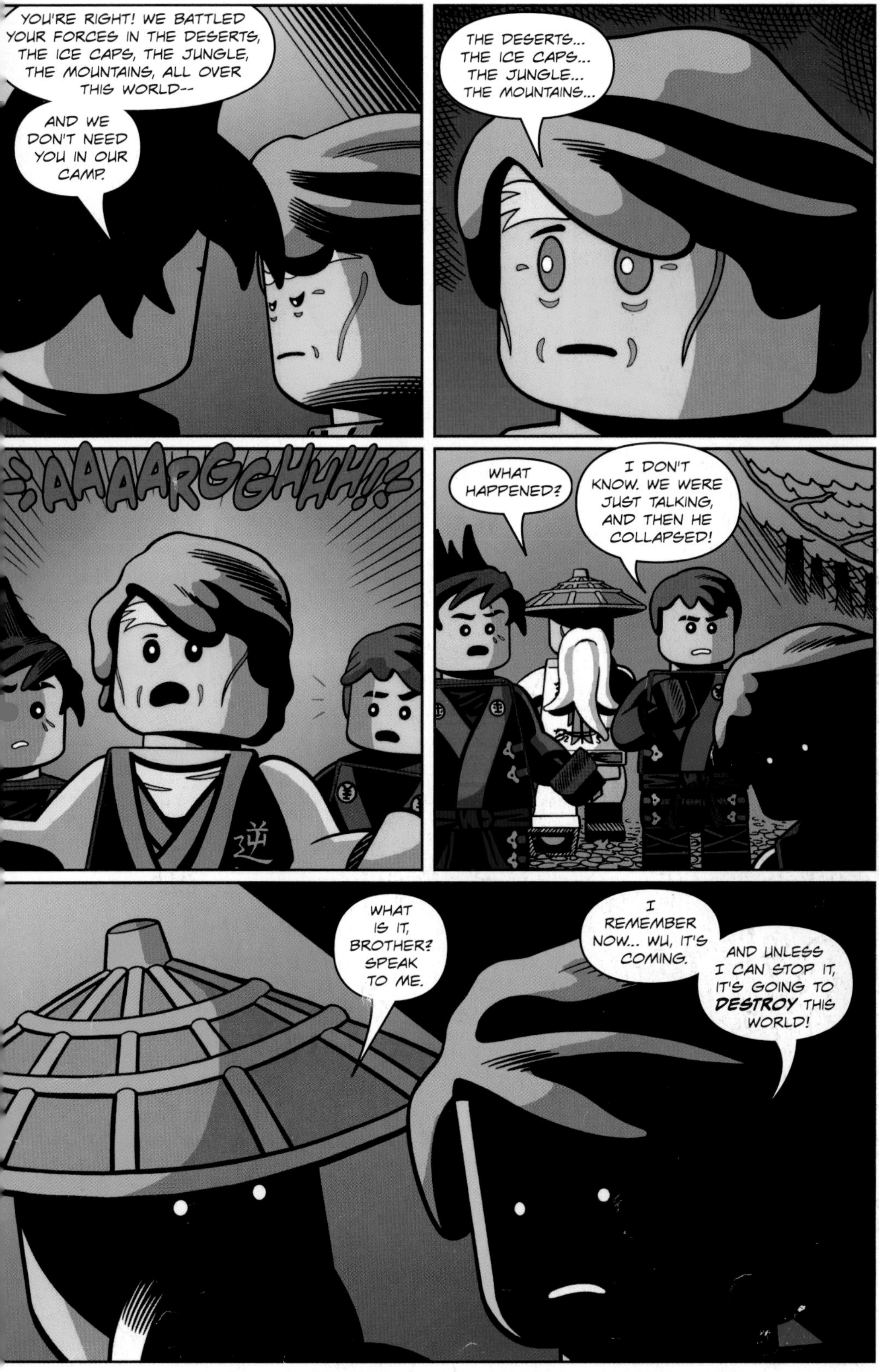
YOU'RE RIGHT! WE BATTLED YOUR FORCES IN THE DESERTS, THE ICE CAPS, THE JUNGLE, THE MOUNTAINS, ALL OVER THIS WORLD--
AND WE DON'T NEED YOU IN OUR CAMP.
THE DESERTS... THE ICE CAPS... THE JUNGLE... THE MOUNTAINS...
AAAARGGHHH!!
WHAT HAPPENED?
I DON'T KNOW. WE WERE JUST TALKING, AND THEN HE COLLAPSED!
WHAT IS IT, BROTHER? SPEAK TO ME.
I REMEMBER NOW... WU, IT'S COMING.
AND UNLESS I CAN STOP IT, IT'S GOING TO DESTROY THIS WORLD!

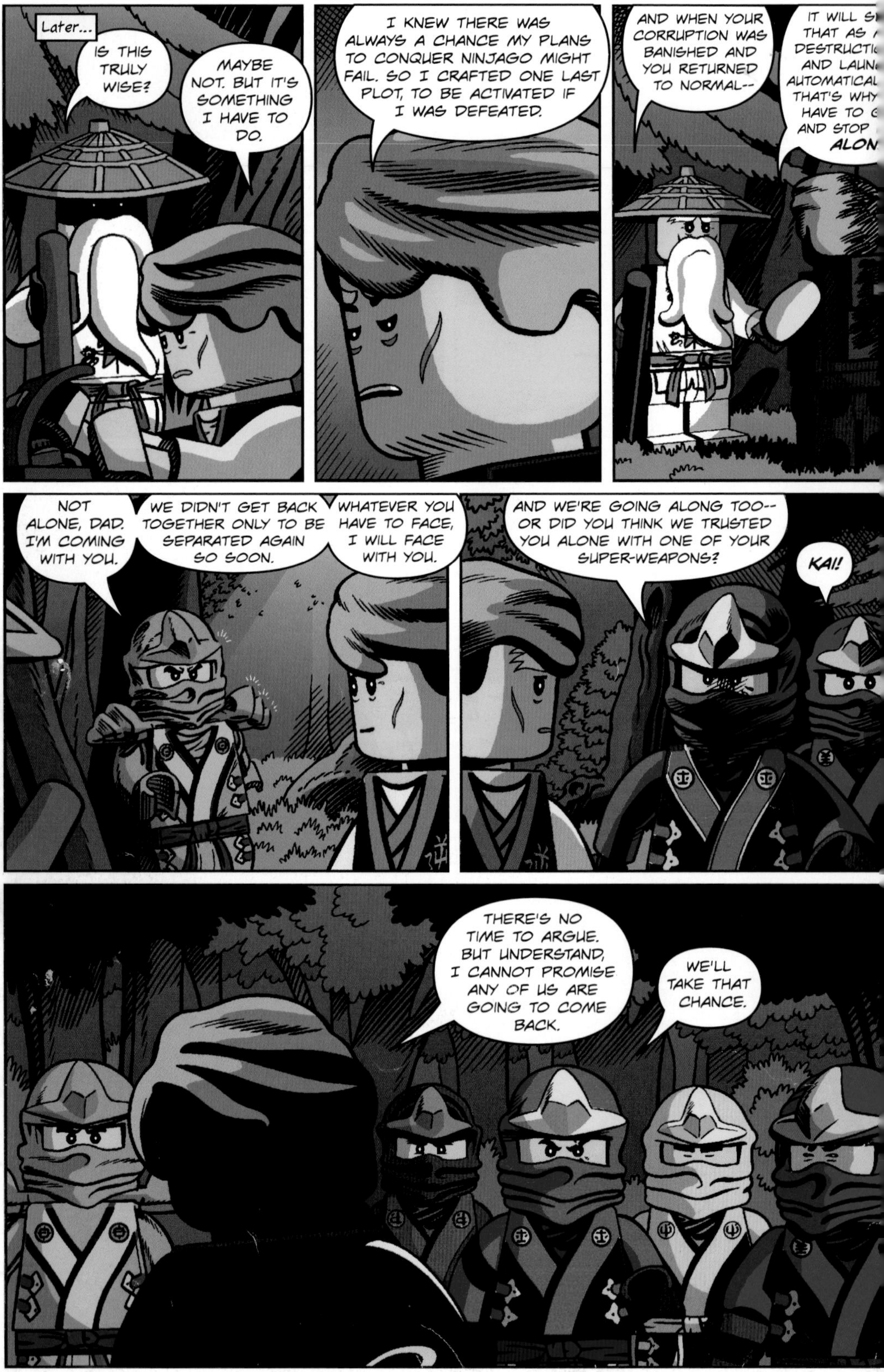
Later...
IS THIS TRULY WISE?
MAYBE NOT. BUT IT'S SOMETHING I HAVE TO DO.
I KNEW THERE WAS ALWAYS A CHANCE MY PLANS TO CONQUER NINJAGO MIGHT FAIL. SO I CRAFTED ONE LAST PLOT, TO BE ACTIVATED IF I WAS DEFEATED.
AND WHEN YOUR CORRUPTION WAS BANISHED AND YOU RETURNED TO NORMAL--
NOT ALONE, DAD. I'M COMING WITH YOU.
WE DIDN'T GET BACK TOGETHER ONLY TO BE SEPARATED AGAIN SO SOON.
WHATEVER YOU HAVE TO FACE, I WILL FACE WITH YOU.
AND WE'RE GOING ALONG TOO-- OR DID YOU THINK WE TRUSTED YOU ALONE WITH ONE OF YOUR SUPER-WEAPONS?
KAI!
THERE'S NO TIME TO ARGUE. BUT UNDERSTAND, I CANNOT PROMISE ANY OF US ARE GOING TO COME BACK.
WE'LL TAKE THAT CHANCE.

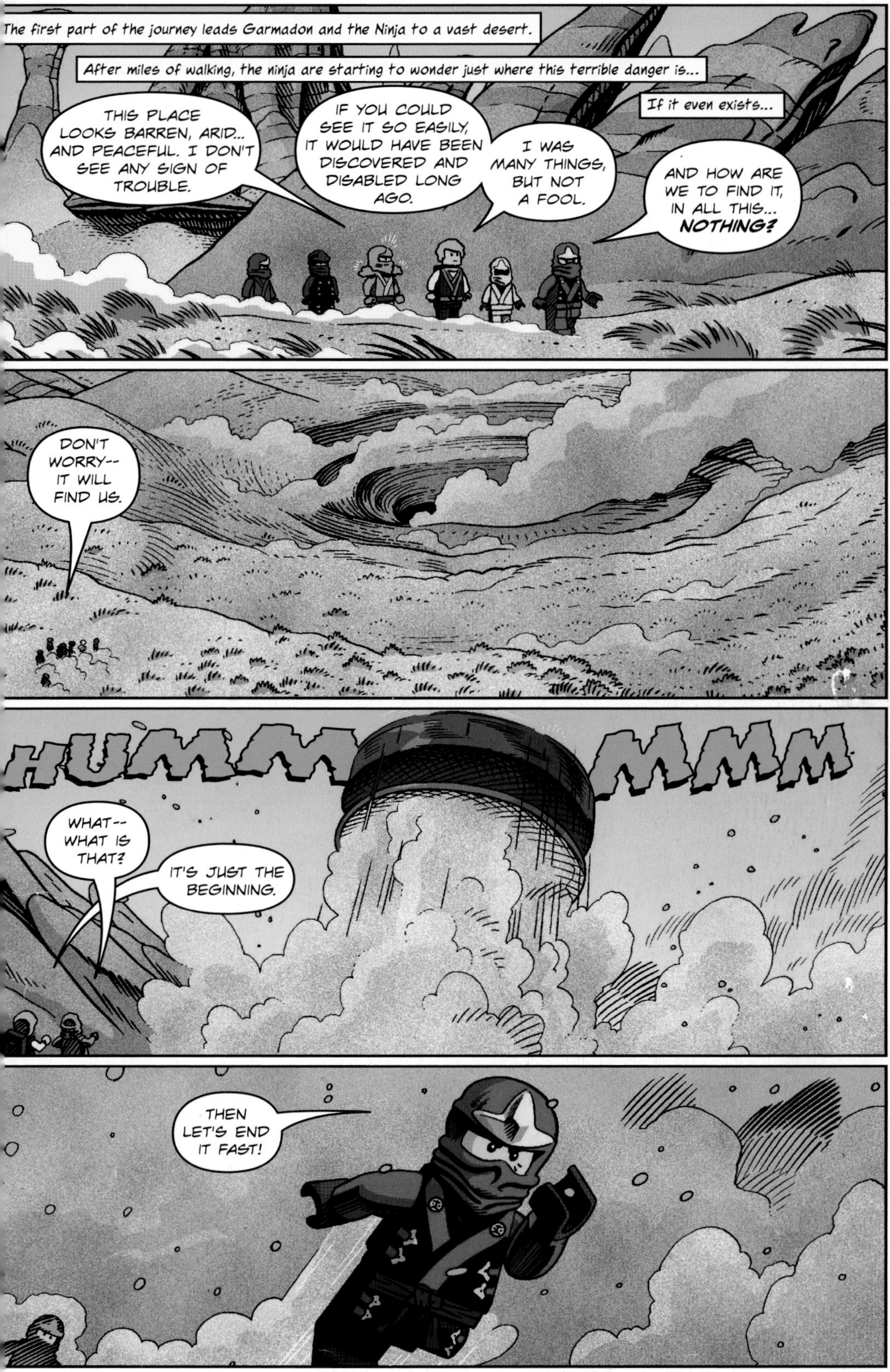
The first part of the journey leads Garmadon and the Ninja to a vast desert.
After miles of walking, the ninja are starting to wonder just where this terrible danger is...
If it even exists...
THIS PLACE LOOKS BARREN, ARID... AND PEACEFUL. I DON'T SEE ANY SIGN OF TROUBLE.
IF YOU COULD SEE IT SO EASILY, IT WOULD HAVE BEEN DISCOVERED AND DISABLED LONG AGO.
I WAS MANY THINGS, BUT NOT A FOOL.
AND HOW ARE WE TO FIND IT, IN ALL THIS... NOTHING?
DON'T WORRY-- IT WILL FIND US.
HUMMMMMM
WHAT-- WHAT IS THAT?
IT'S JUST THE BEGINNING.
THEN LET'S END IT FAST!

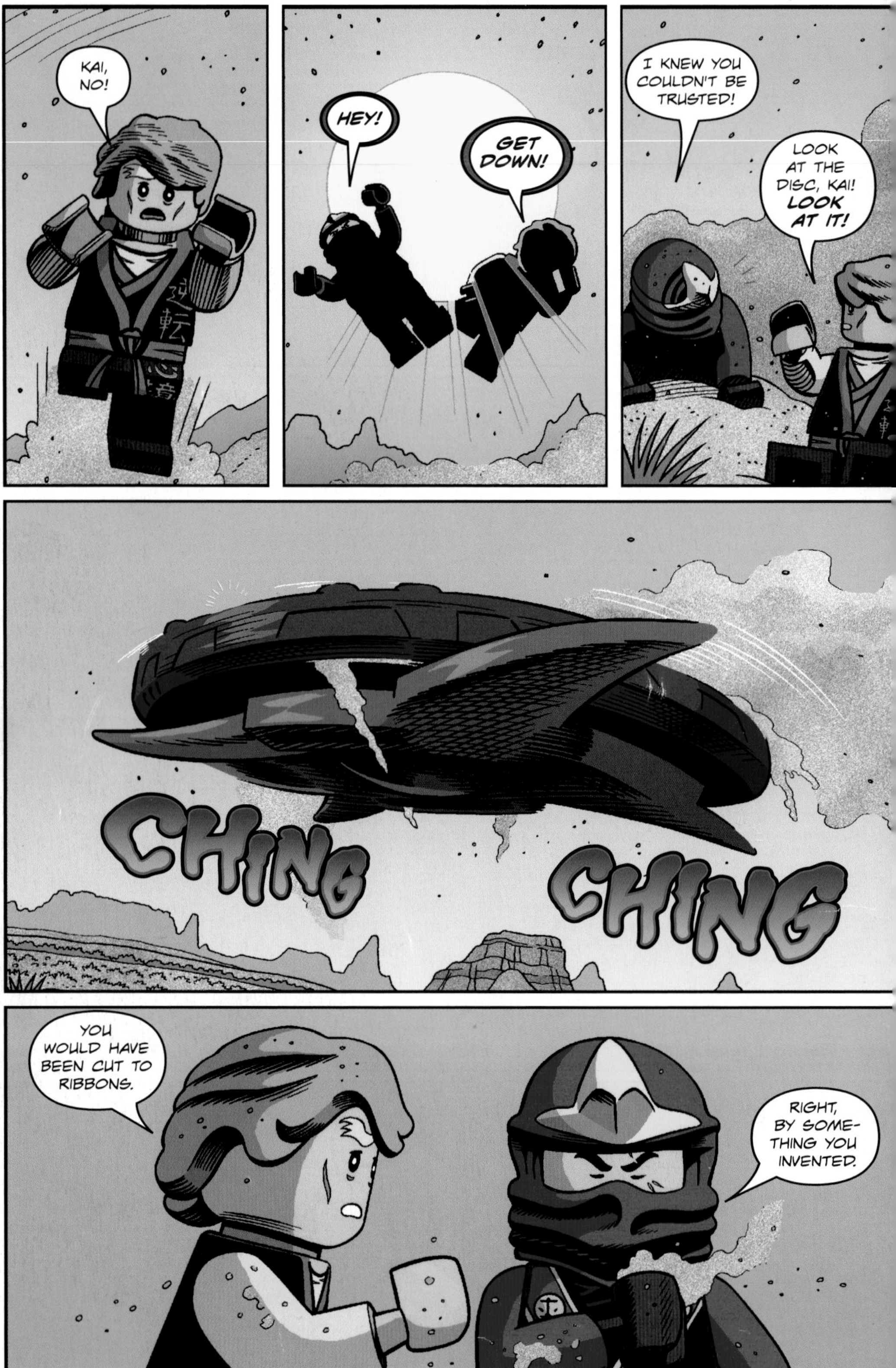
KAI, NO!
HEY!
GET DOWN!
I KNEW YOU COULDN'T BE TRUSTED!
LOOK AT THE DISC, KAI! **LOOK AT IT!**
CHING
CHING
YOU WOULD HAVE BEEN CUT TO RIBBONS.
RIGHT, BY SOME-THING YOU INVENTED.

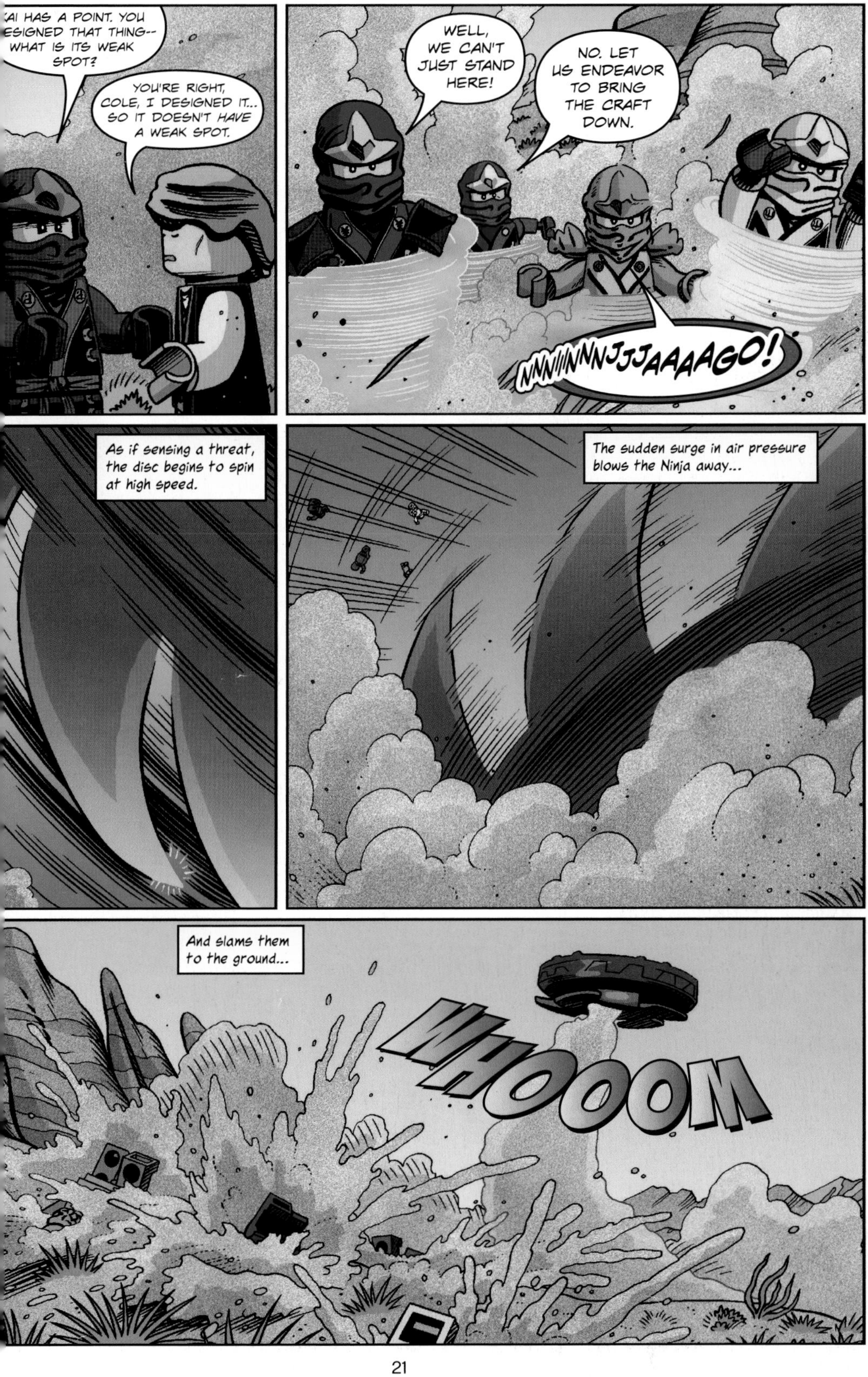

KAI HAS A POINT. YOU DESIGNED THAT THING-- WHAT IS ITS WEAK SPOT?
YOU'RE RIGHT, COLE, I DESIGNED IT... SO IT DOESN'T HAVE A WEAK SPOT.
WELL, WE CAN'T JUST STAND HERE!
NO. LET US ENDEAVOR TO BRING THE CRAFT DOWN.
NNNINNNJJAAAAGO!
As if sensing a threat, the disc begins to spin at high speed.
The sudden surge in air pressure blows the Ninja away...
And slams them to the ground...
WHOOOM

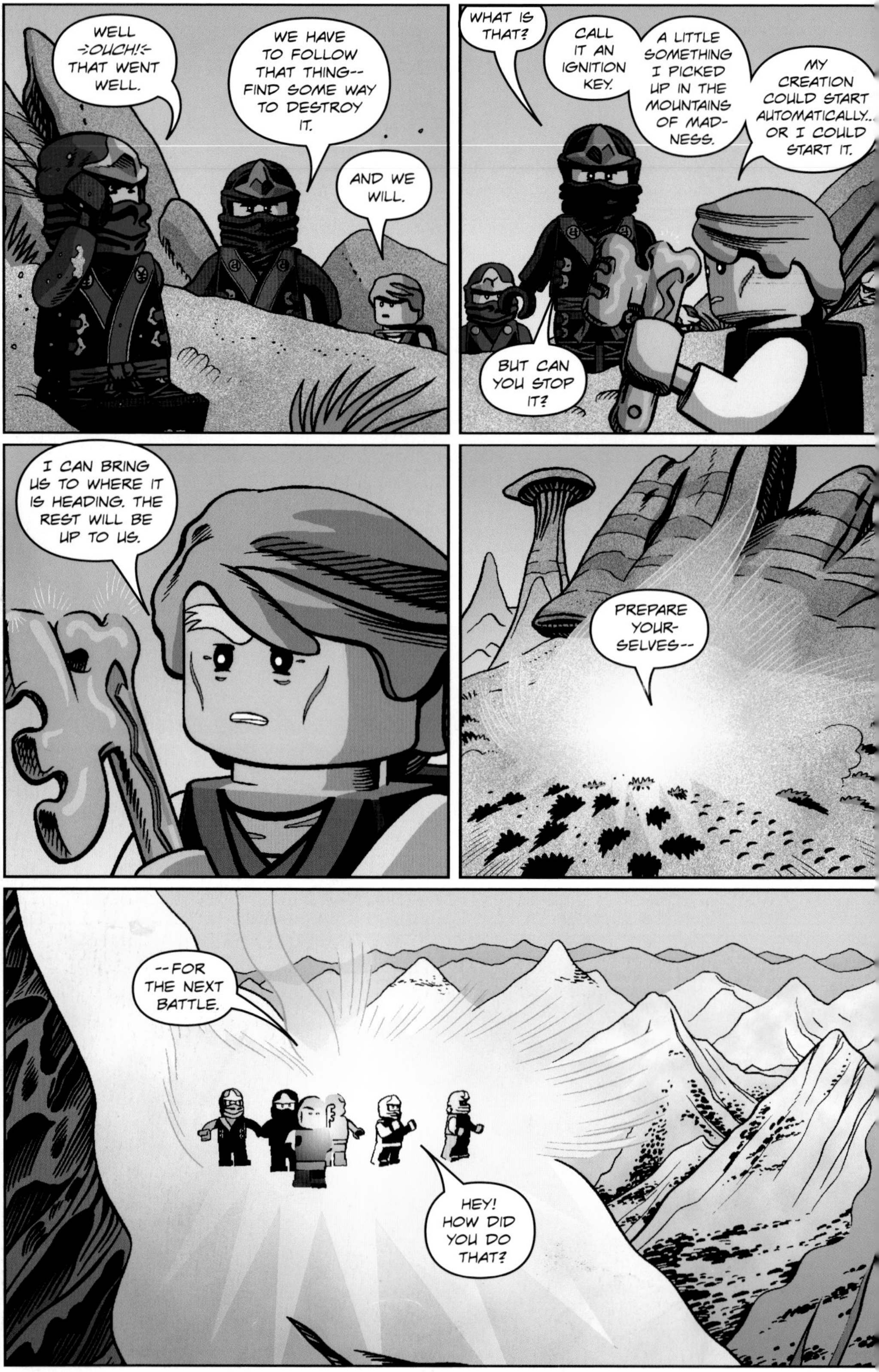
WELL
-OUCH!-
THAT WENT
WELL.
WE HAVE
TO FOLLOW
THAT THING--
FIND SOME WAY
TO DESTROY
IT.
AND WE
WILL.
WHAT IS
THAT?
CALL
IT AN
IGNITION
KEY.
A LITTLE
SOMETHING
I PICKED
UP IN THE
MOUNTAINS
OF MAD-
NESS.
MY
CREATION
COULD START
AUTOMATICALLY...
OR I COULD
START IT.
BUT CAN
YOU STOP
IT?
I CAN BRING
US TO WHERE IT
IS HEADING. THE
REST WILL BE
UP TO US.
PREPARE
YOUR-
SELVES--
--FOR
THE NEXT
BATTLE.
HEY!
HOW DID
YOU DO
THAT?

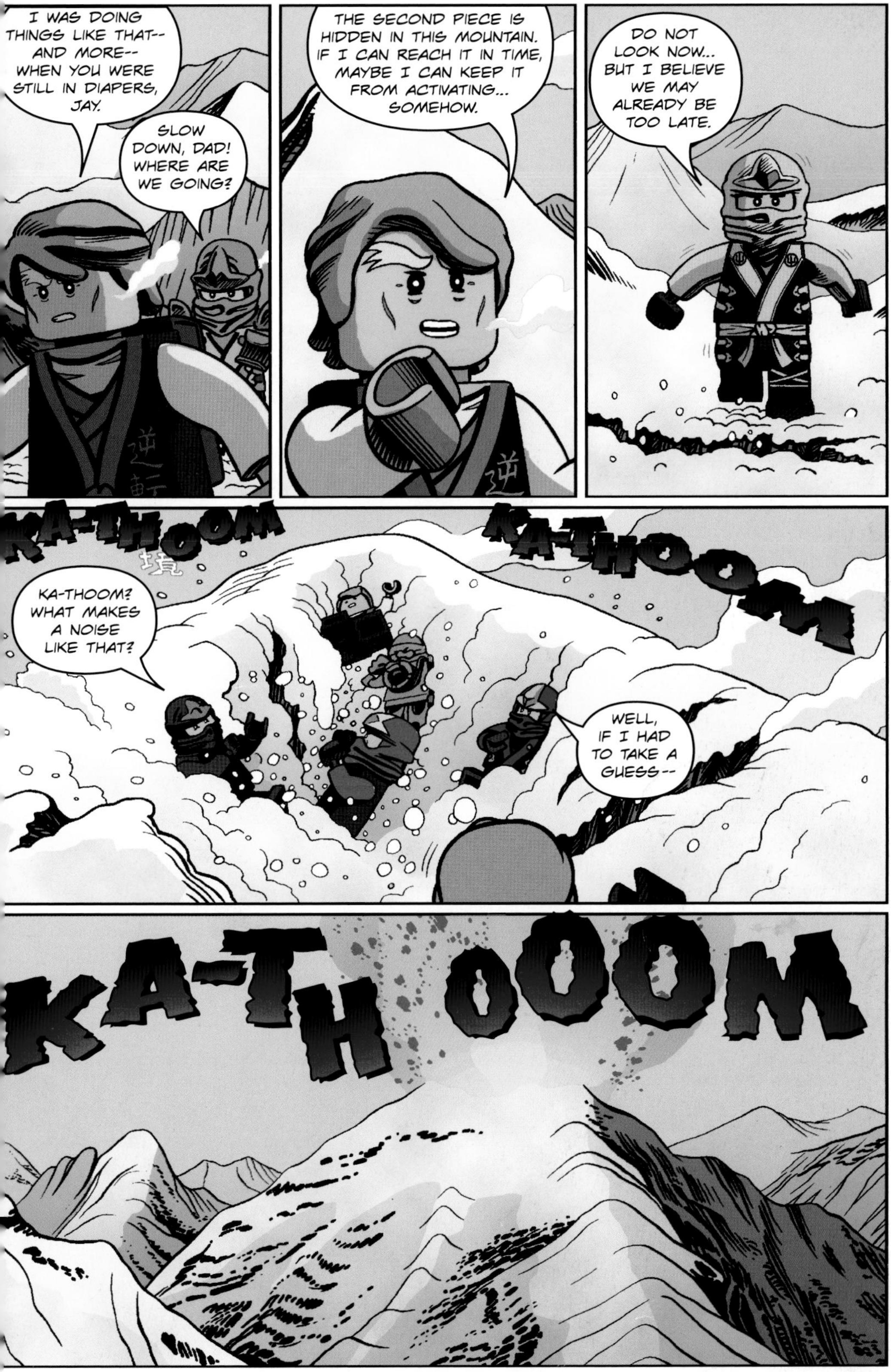
I WAS DOING THINGS LIKE THAT-- AND MORE-- WHEN YOU WERE STILL IN DIAPERS, JAY.
SLOW DOWN, DAD! WHERE ARE WE GOING?
THE SECOND PIECE IS HIDDEN IN THIS MOUNTAIN. IF I CAN REACH IT IN TIME, MAYBE I CAN KEEP IT FROM ACTIVATING... SOMEHOW.
DO NOT LOOK NOW... BUT I BELIEVE WE MAY ALREADY BE TOO LATE.
KA-THOOM
KA-THOOM
KA-THOOM? WHAT MAKES A NOISE LIKE THAT?
WELL, IF I HAD TO TAKE A GUESS--
KA-THOOOM

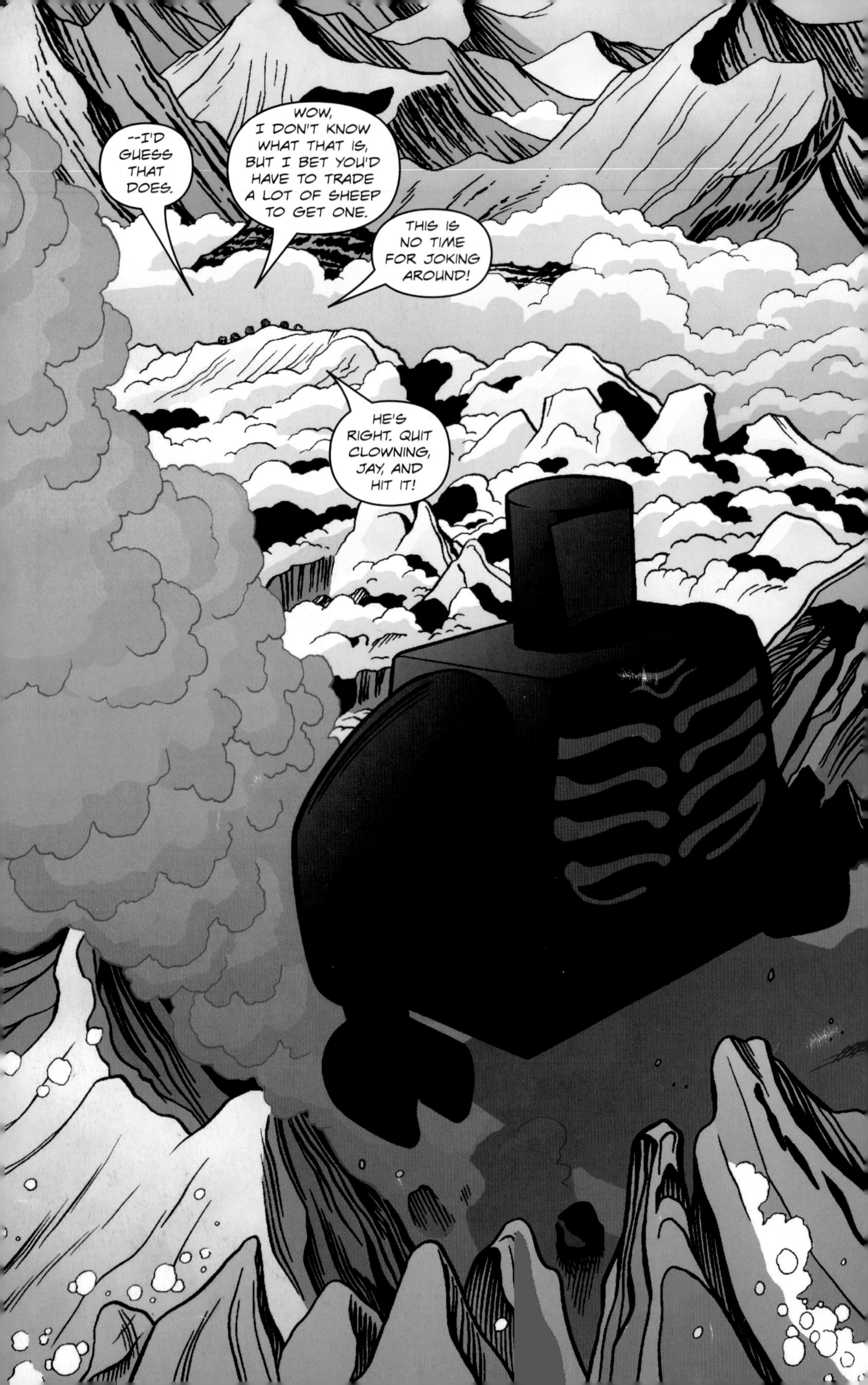
--I'D GUESS THAT DOES.
WOW, I DON'T KNOW WHAT THAT IS, BUT I BET YOU'D HAVE TO TRADE A LOT OF SHEEP TO GET ONE.
THIS IS NO TIME FOR JOKING AROUND!
HE'S RIGHT. QUIT CLOWNING, JAY, AND HIT IT!

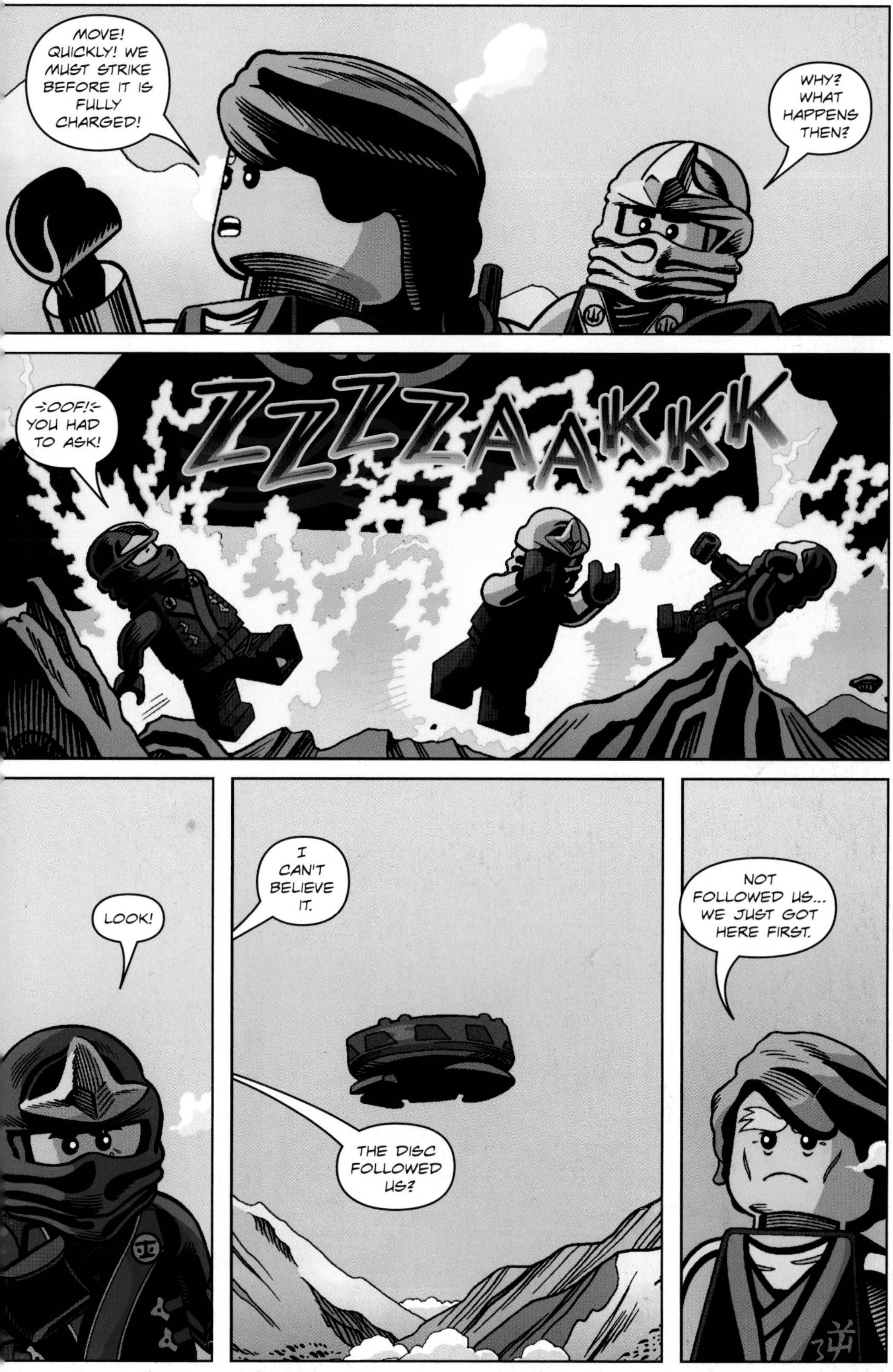
MOVE! QUICKLY! WE MUST STRIKE BEFORE IT IS FULLY CHARGED!
WHY? WHAT HAPPENS THEN?
ZZZZAAKKK
>OOF!< YOU HAD TO ASK!
LOOK!
I CAN'T BELIEVE IT.
THE DISC FOLLOWED US?
NOT FOLLOWED US... WE JUST GOT HERE FIRST.

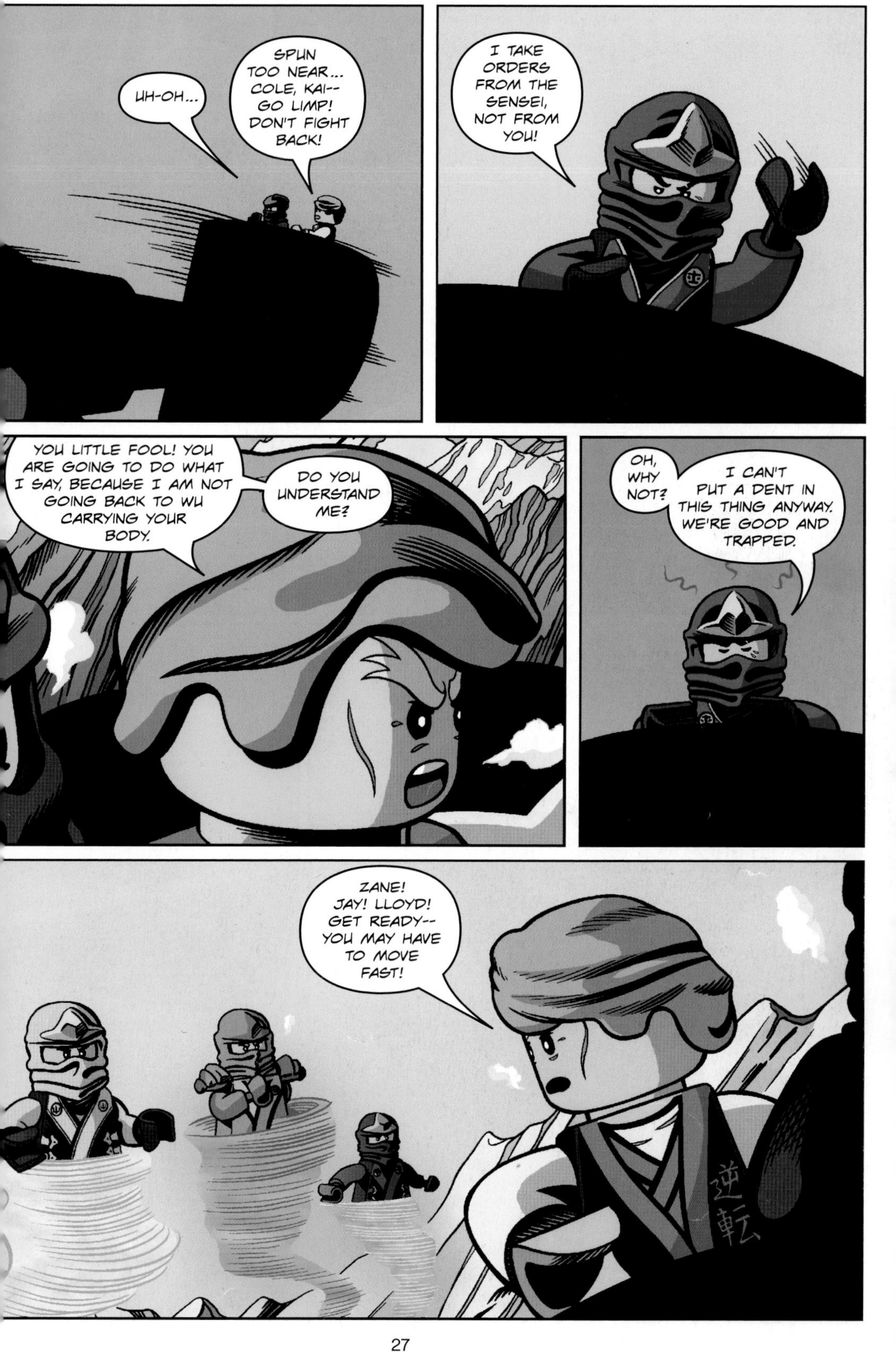
UH-OH...
SPUN TOO NEAR... COLE, KAI-- GO LIMP! DON'T FIGHT BACK!
I TAKE ORDERS FROM THE SENSEI, NOT FROM YOU!
YOU LITTLE FOOL! YOU ARE GOING TO DO WHAT I SAY, BECAUSE I AM NOT GOING BACK TO WU CARRYING YOUR BODY.
DO YOU UNDERSTAND ME?
OH, WHY NOT?
I CAN'T PUT A DENT IN THIS THING ANYWAY. WE'RE GOOD AND TRAPPED.
ZANE! JAY! LLOYD! GET READY-- YOU MAY HAVE TO MOVE FAST!
逆転

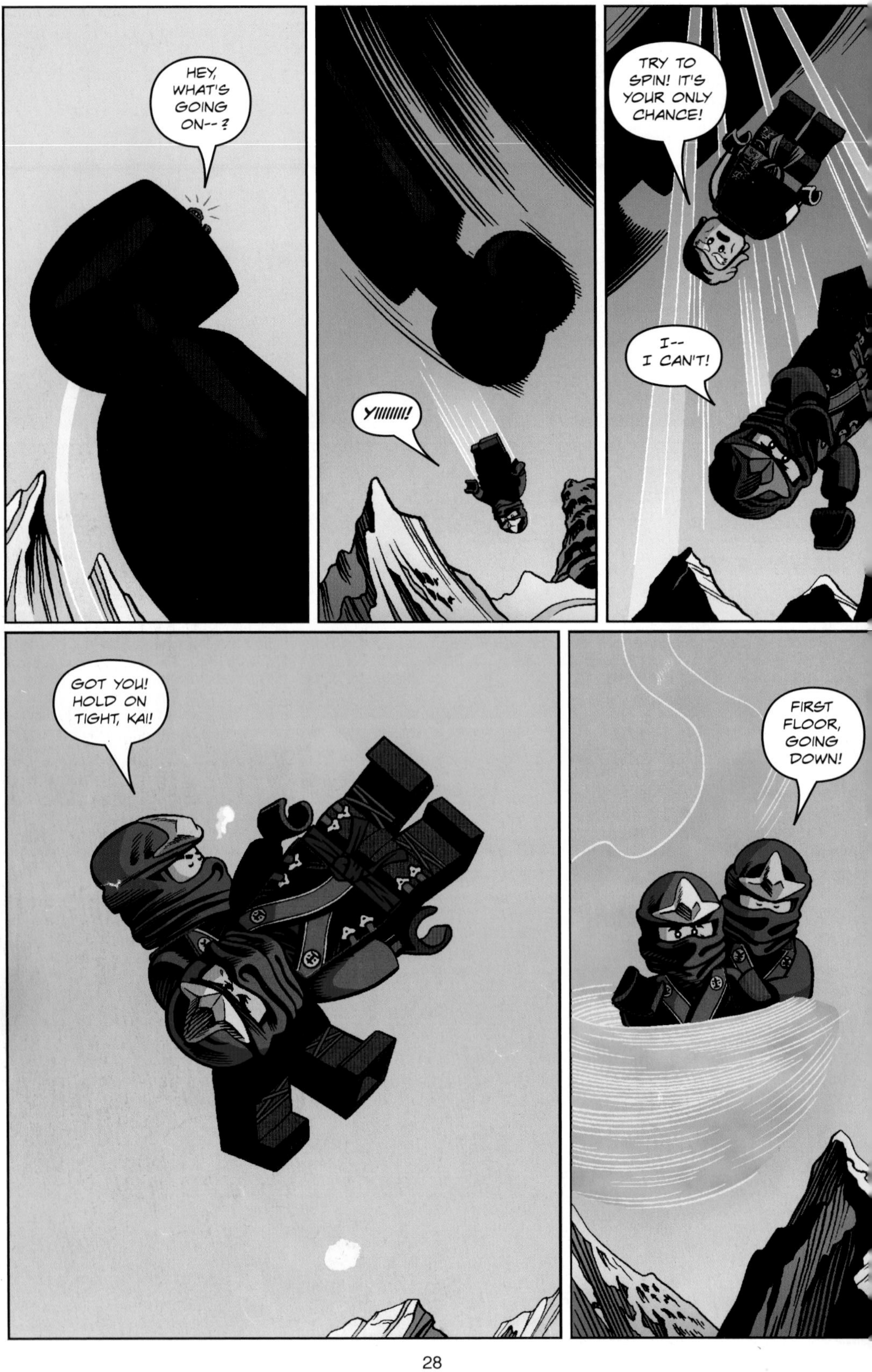
HEY, WHAT'S GOING ON--?
YIIIIIII!
TRY TO SPIN! IT'S YOUR ONLY CHANCE!
I-- I CAN'T!
GOT YOU! HOLD ON TIGHT, KAI!
FIRST FLOOR, GOING DOWN!

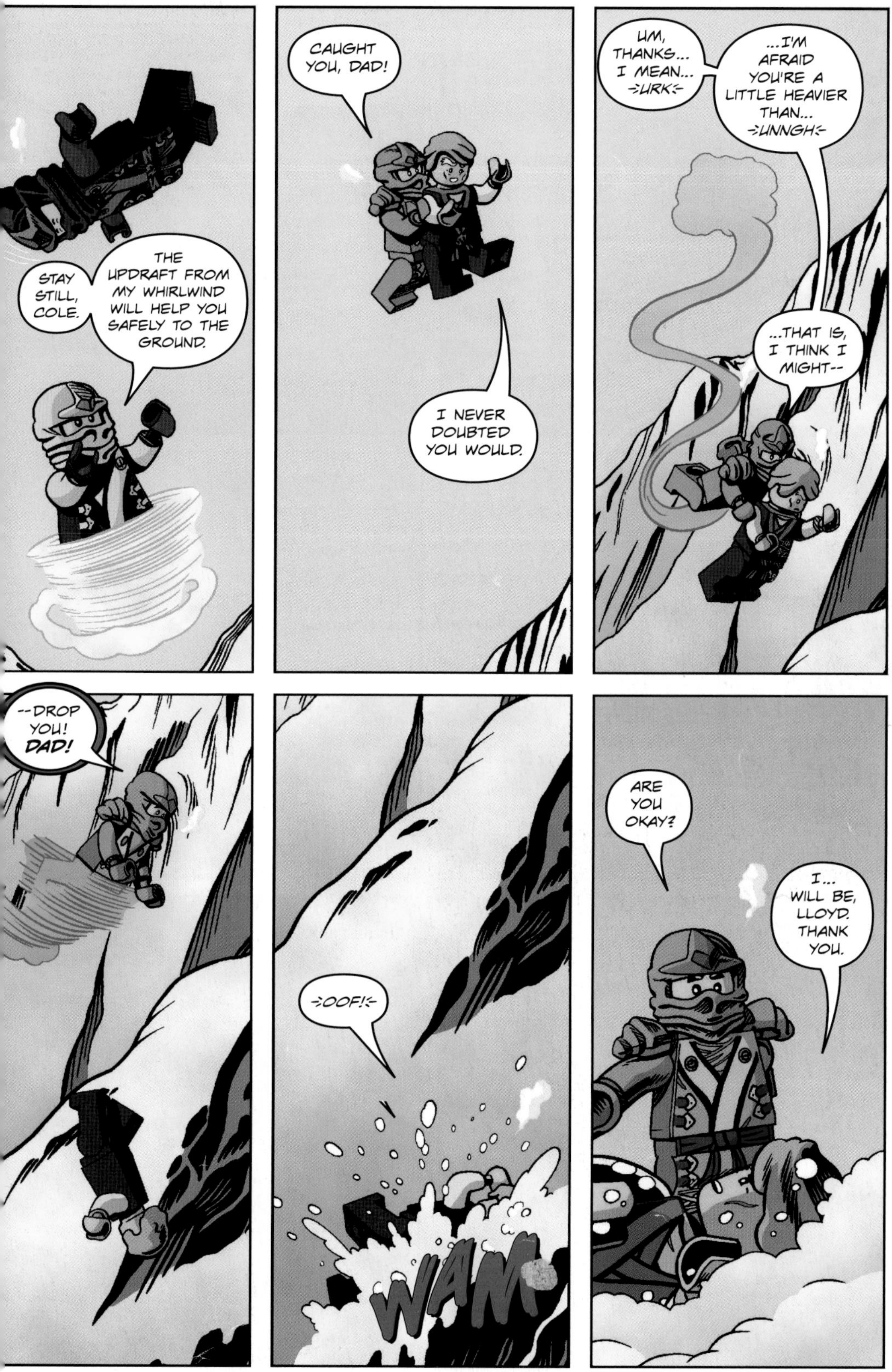
STAY STILL, COLE.
THE UPDRAFT FROM MY WHIRLWIND WILL HELP YOU SAFELY TO THE GROUND.
CAUGHT YOU, DAD!
I NEVER DOUBTED YOU WOULD.
UM, THANKS... I MEAN... URK
...I'M AFRAID YOU'RE A LITTLE HEAVIER THAN... UNNGH
...THAT IS, I THINK I MIGHT--
--DROP YOU! DAD!
OOF!
WAM
ARE YOU OKAY?
I... WILL BE, LLOYD. THANK YOU.

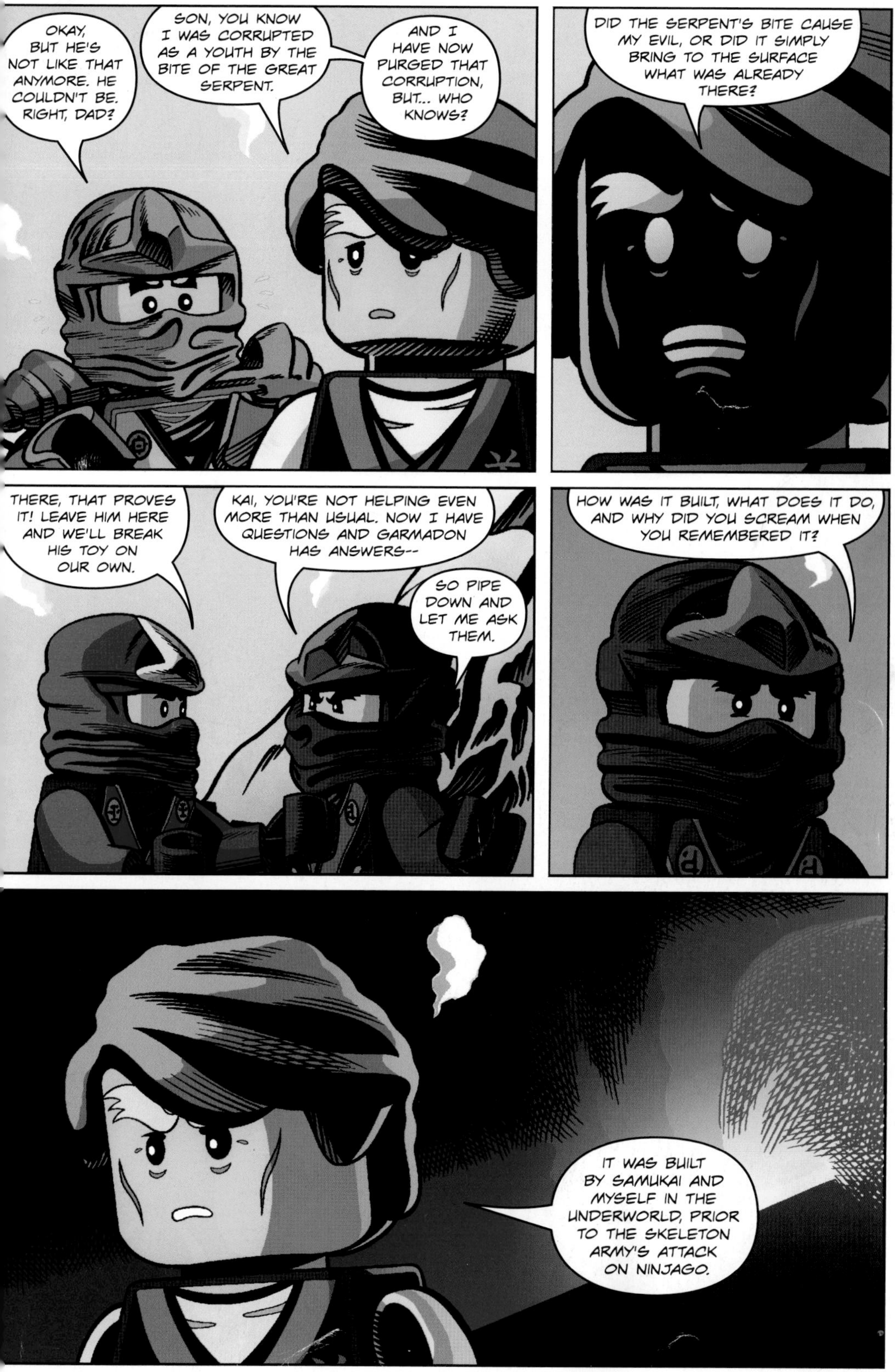

OKAY, BUT HE'S NOT LIKE THAT ANYMORE. HE COULDN'T BE. RIGHT, DAD?
SON, YOU KNOW I WAS CORRUPTED AS A YOUTH BY THE BITE OF THE GREAT SERPENT.
AND I HAVE NOW PURGED THAT CORRUPTION, BUT... WHO KNOWS?
DID THE SERPENT'S BITE CAUSE MY EVIL, OR DID IT SIMPLY BRING TO THE SURFACE WHAT WAS ALREADY THERE?
THERE, THAT PROVES IT! LEAVE HIM HERE AND WE'LL BREAK HIS TOY ON OUR OWN.
KAI, YOU'RE NOT HELPING EVEN MORE THAN USUAL. NOW I HAVE QUESTIONS AND GARMADON HAS ANSWERS--
SO PIPE DOWN AND LET ME ASK THEM.
HOW WAS IT BUILT, WHAT DOES IT DO, AND WHY DID YOU SCREAM WHEN YOU REMEMBERED IT?
IT WAS BUILT BY SAMUKAI AND MYSELF IN THE UNDERWORLD, PRIOR TO THE SKELETON ARMY'S ATTACK ON NINJAGO.

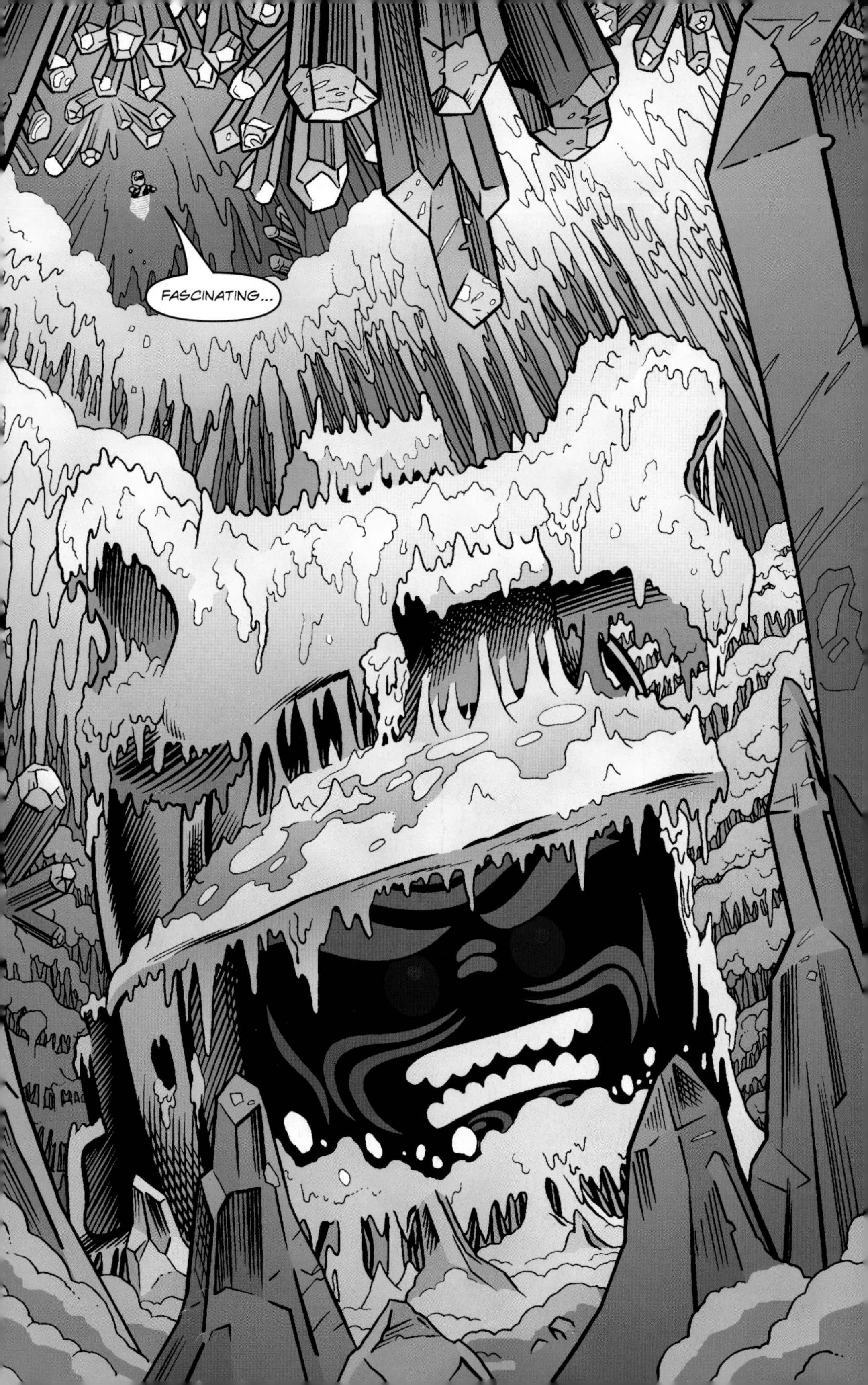
FASCINATING...

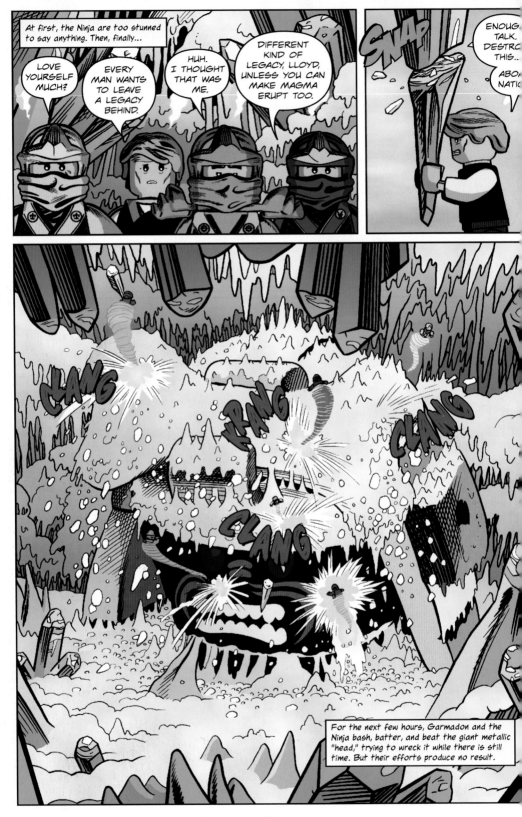

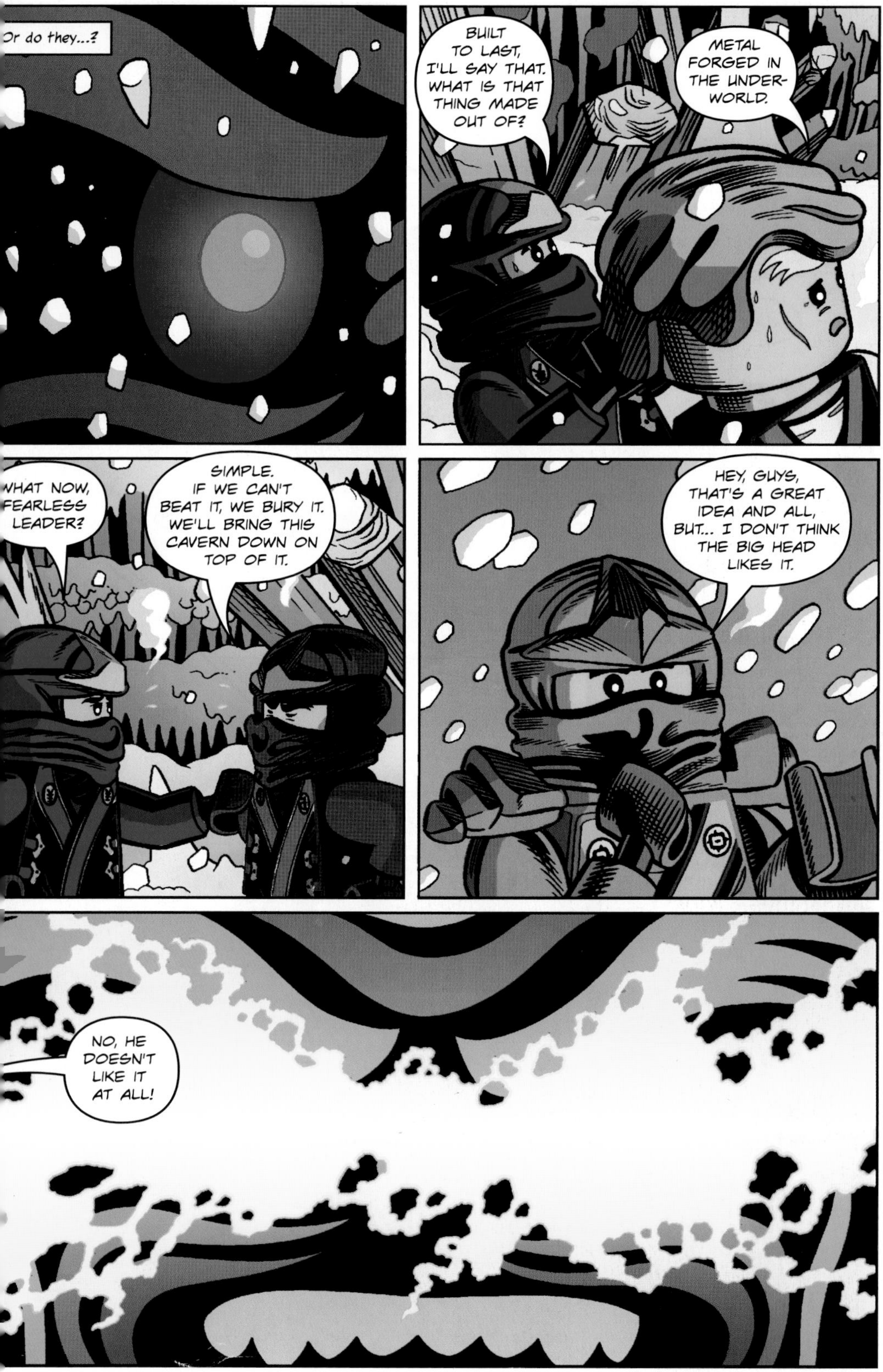
Or do they...?
BUILT TO LAST, I'LL SAY THAT. WHAT IS THAT THING MADE OUT OF?
METAL FORGED IN THE UNDER-WORLD.
WHAT NOW, FEARLESS LEADER?
SIMPLE. IF WE CAN'T BEAT IT, WE BURY IT. WE'LL BRING THIS CAVERN DOWN ON TOP OF IT.
HEY, GUYS, THAT'S A GREAT IDEA AND ALL, BUT... I DON'T THINK THE BIG HEAD LIKES IT.
NO, HE DOESN'T LIKE IT AT ALL!

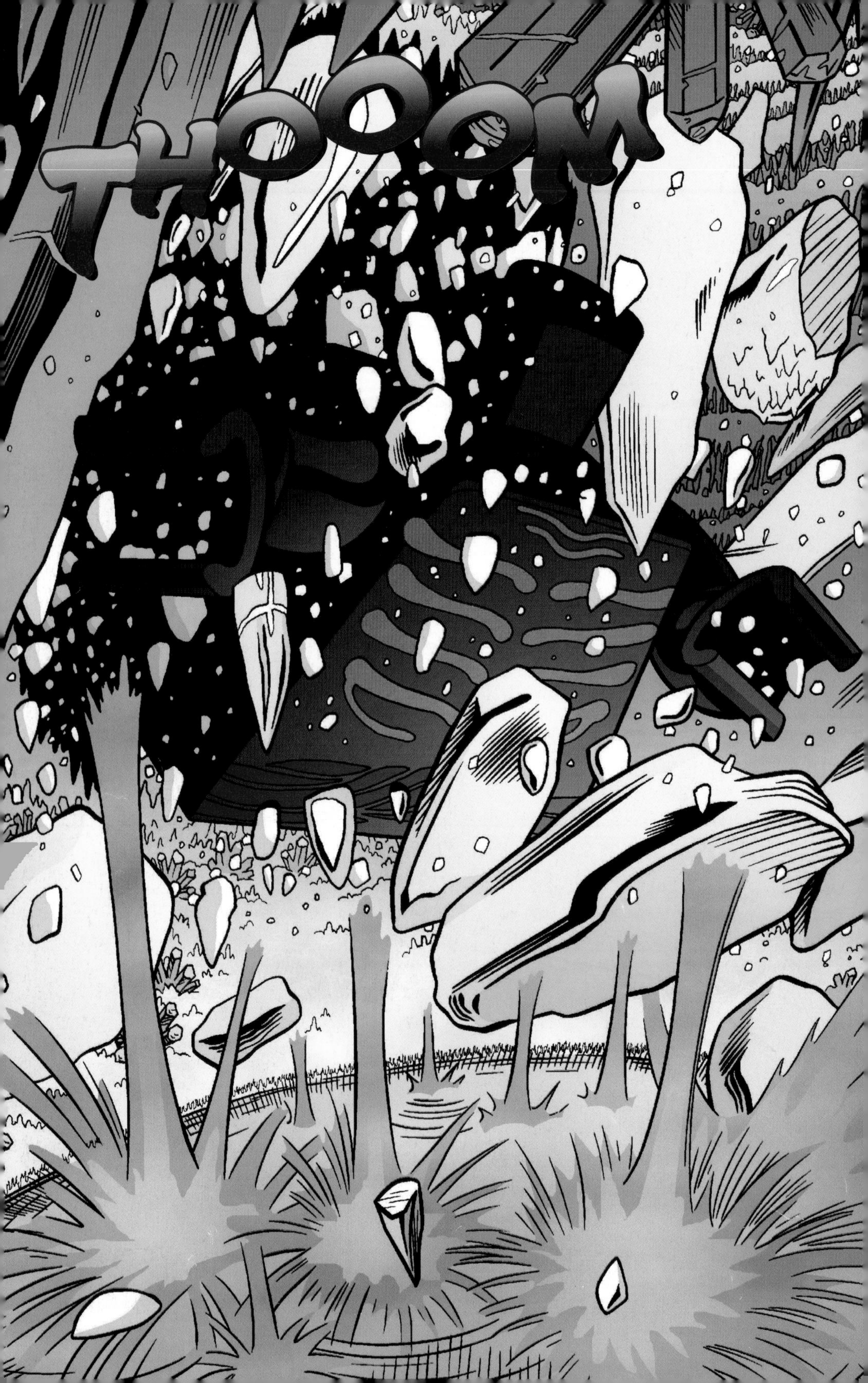
THOOOM

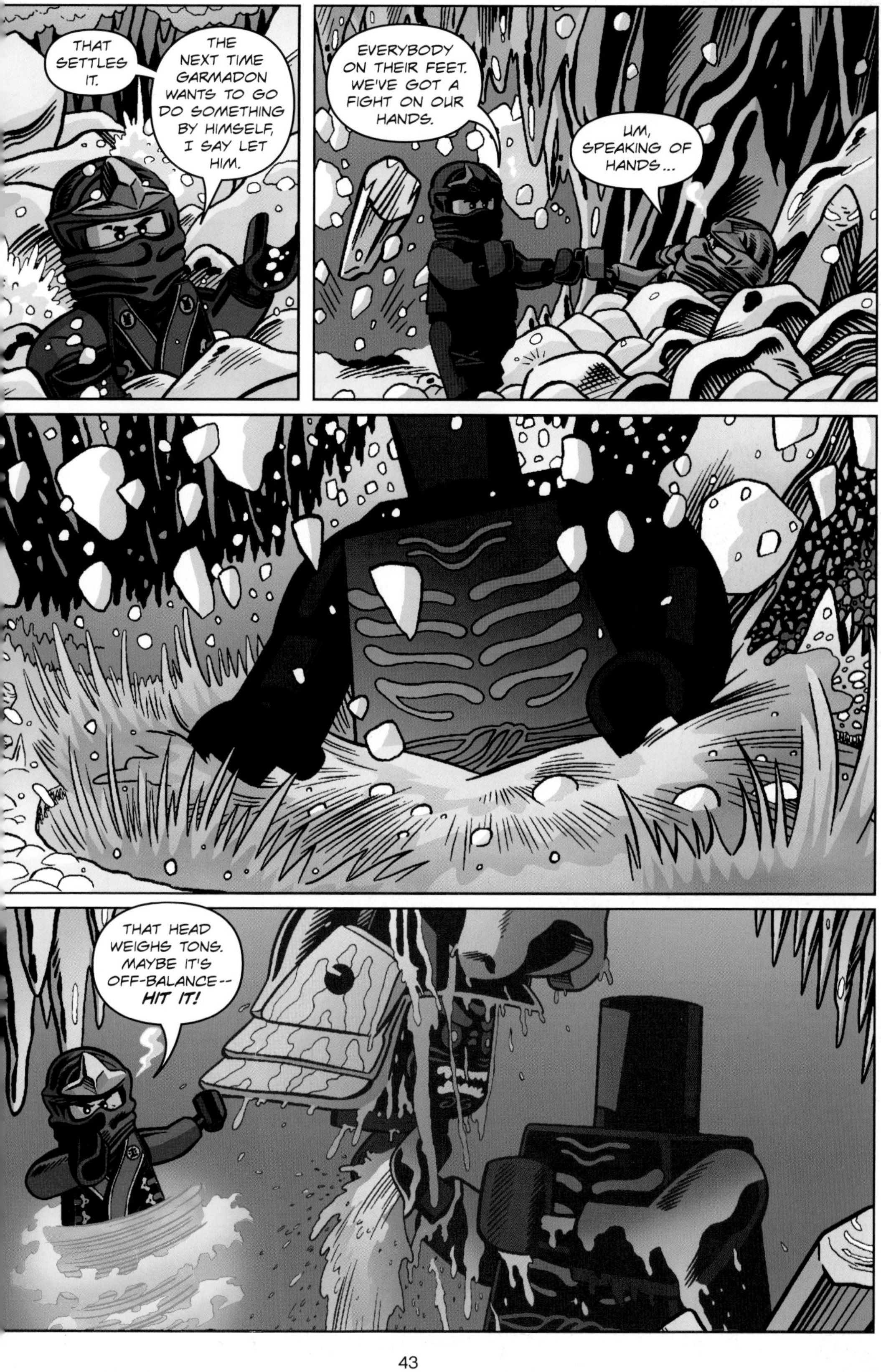
THAT SETTLES IT.
THE NEXT TIME GARMADON WANTS TO GO DO SOMETHING BY HIMSELF, I SAY LET HIM.
EVERYBODY ON THEIR FEET. WE'VE GOT A FIGHT ON OUR HANDS.
UM, SPEAKING OF HANDS...
THAT HEAD WEIGHS TONS. MAYBE IT'S OFF-BALANCE-- ***HIT IT!***

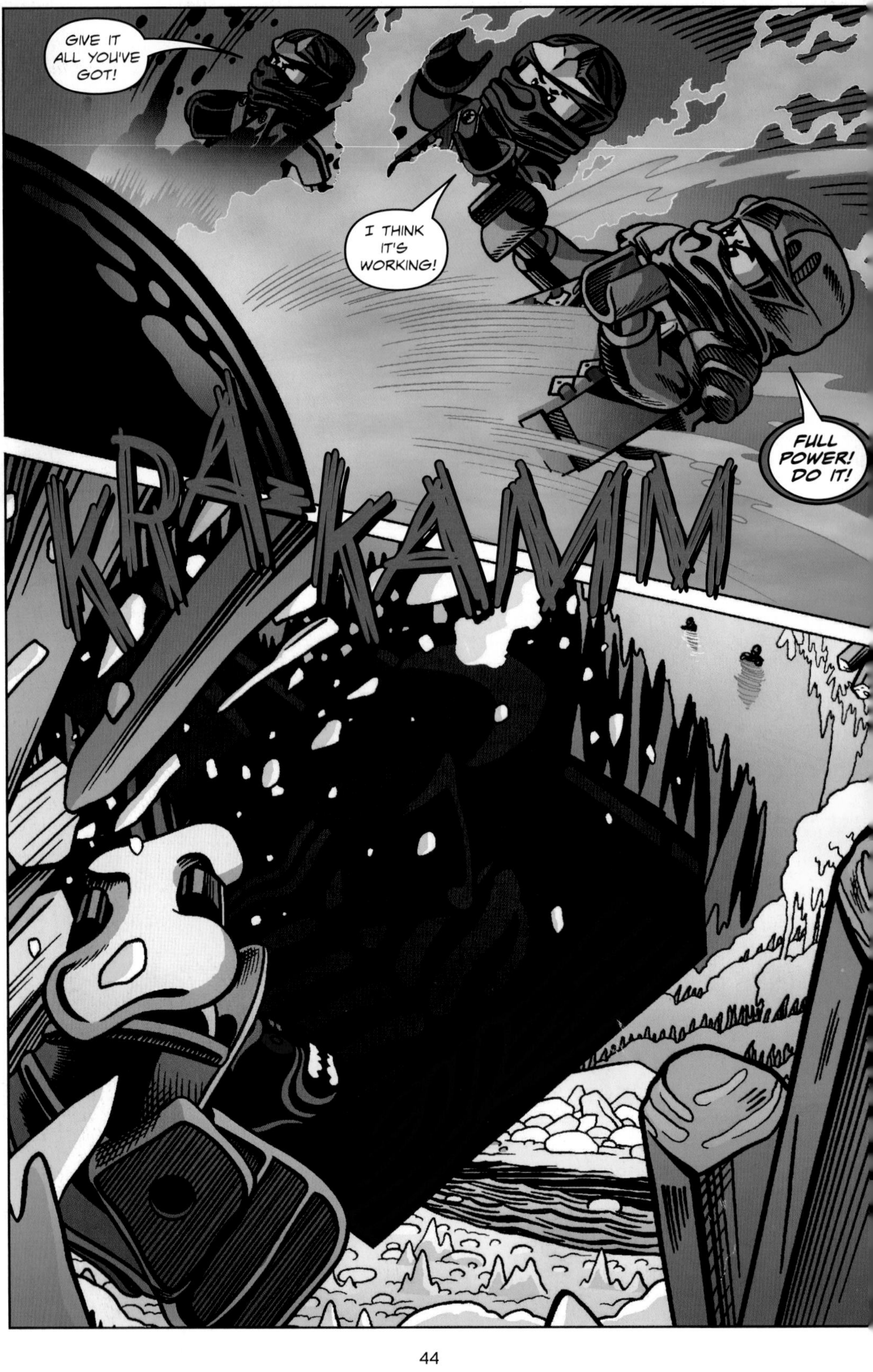
GIVE IT ALL YOU'VE GOT!
I THINK IT'S WORKING!
FULL POWER! DO IT!
KRA-KAMM

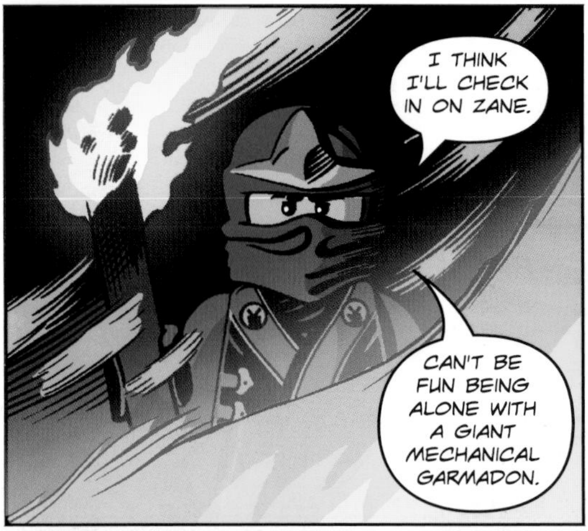
I THINK I'LL CHECK IN ON ZANE.
CAN'T BE FUN BEING ALONE WITH A GIANT MECHANICAL GARMADON.

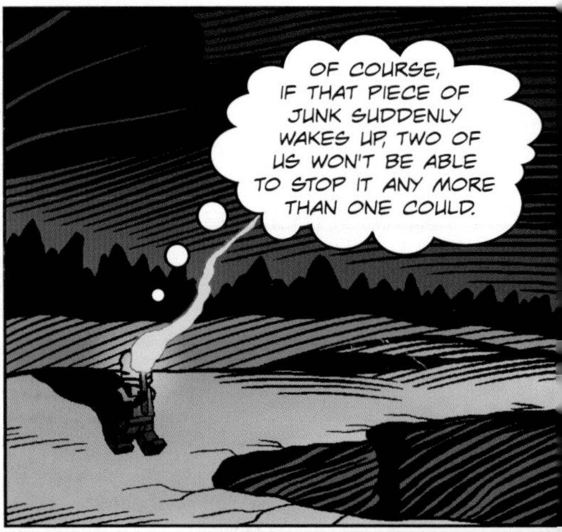
OF COURSE, IF THAT PIECE OF JUNK SUDDENLY WAKES UP, TWO OF US WON'T BE ABLE TO STOP IT ANY MORE THAN ONE COULD.

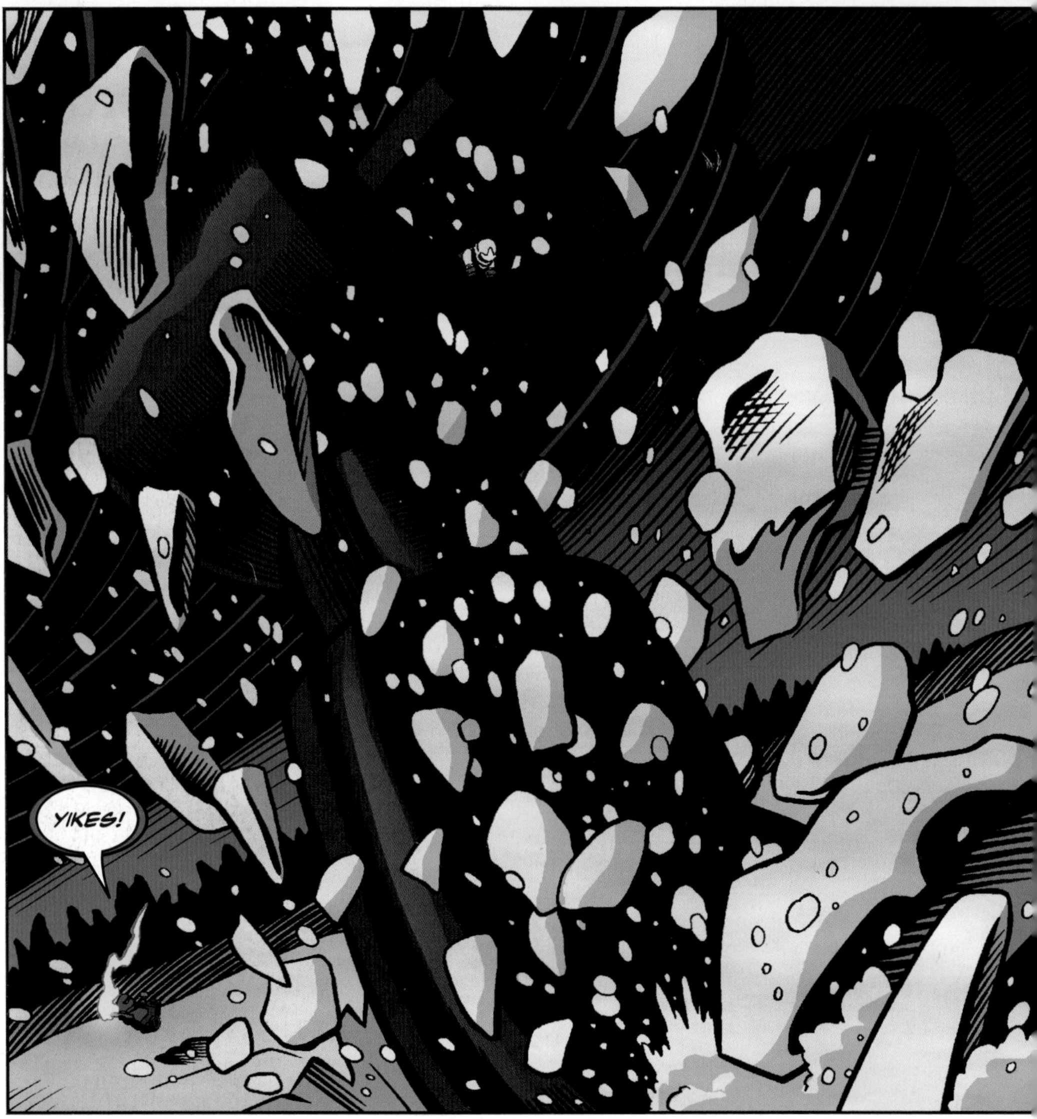
YIKES!

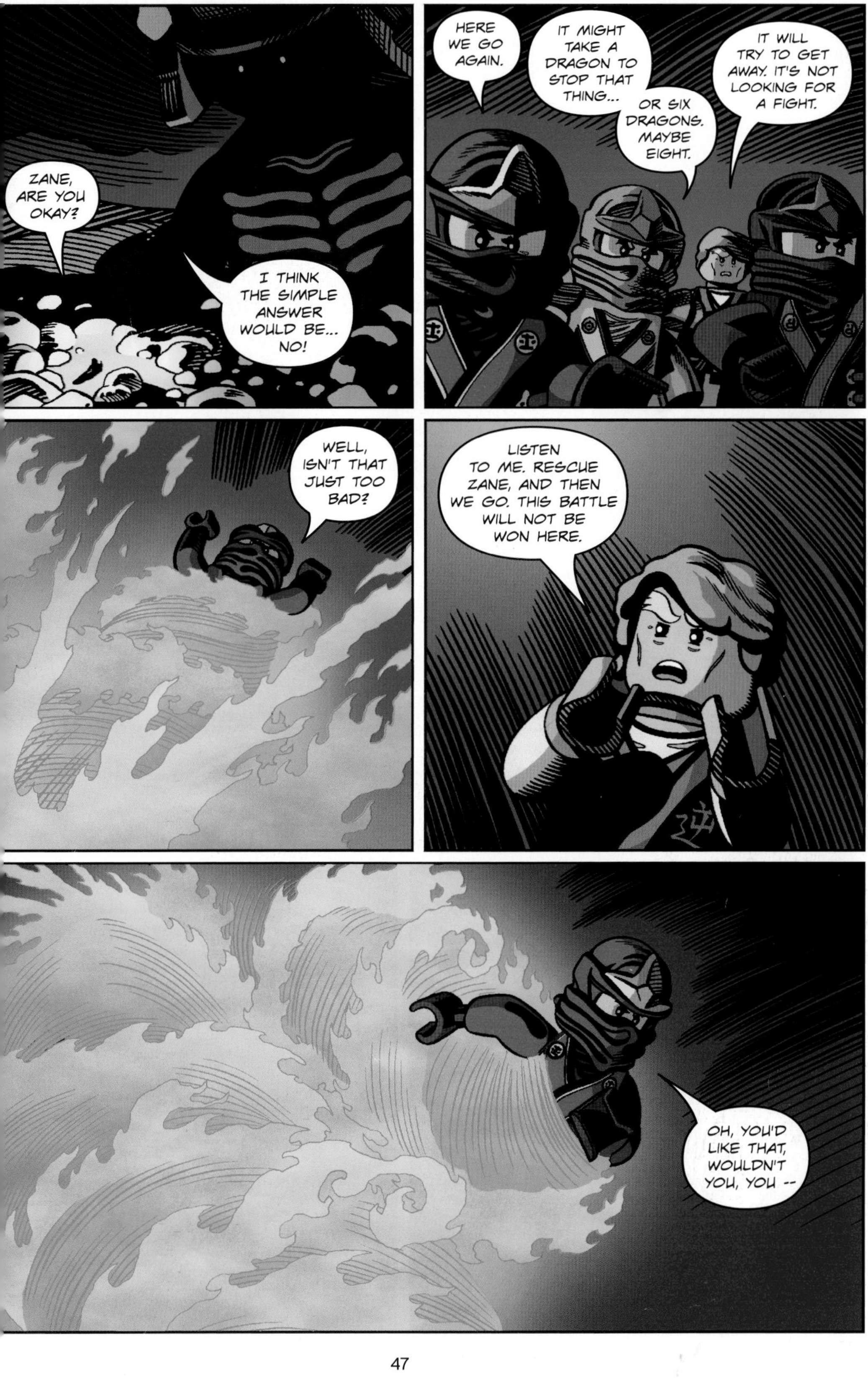
ZANE, ARE YOU OKAY?
I THINK THE SIMPLE ANSWER WOULD BE... NO!
HERE WE GO AGAIN.
IT MIGHT TAKE A DRAGON TO STOP THAT THING...
OR SIX DRAGONS. MAYBE EIGHT.
IT WILL TRY TO GET AWAY. IT'S NOT LOOKING FOR A FIGHT.
WELL, ISN'T THAT JUST TOO BAD?
LISTEN TO ME. RESCUE ZANE, AND THEN WE GO. THIS BATTLE WILL NOT BE WON HERE.
OH, YOU'D LIKE THAT, WOULDN'T YOU, YOU --

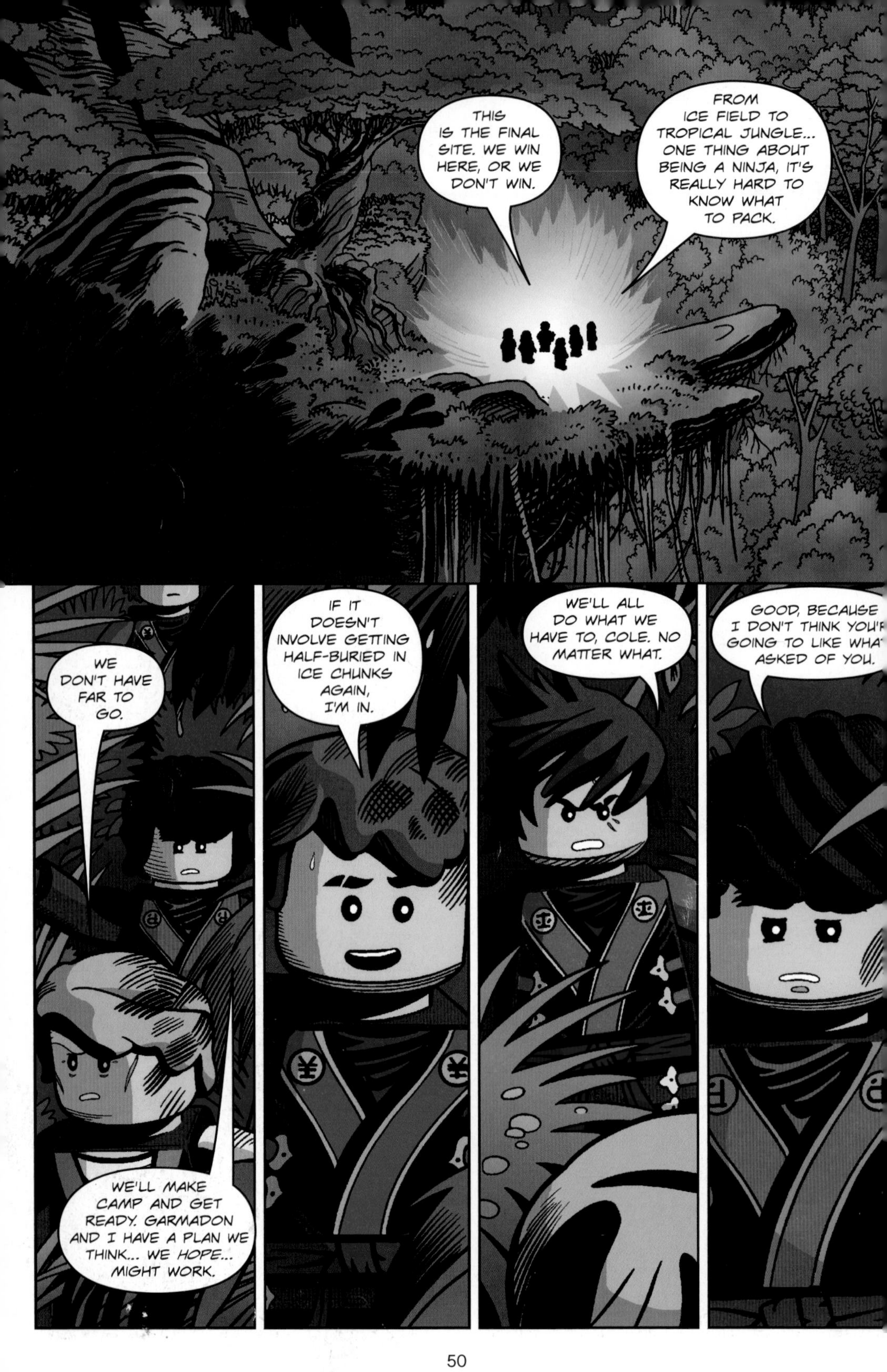
THIS IS THE FINAL SITE. WE WIN HERE, OR WE DON'T WIN.
FROM ICE FIELD TO TROPICAL JUNGLE... ONE THING ABOUT BEING A NINJA, IT'S REALLY HARD TO KNOW WHAT TO PACK.
WE DON'T HAVE FAR TO GO.
WE'LL MAKE CAMP AND GET READY. GARMADON AND I HAVE A PLAN WE THINK... WE *HOPE*... MIGHT WORK.
IF IT DOESN'T INVOLVE GETTING HALF-BURIED IN ICE CHUNKS AGAIN, I'M IN.
WE'LL ALL DO WHAT WE HAVE TO, COLE. NO MATTER WHAT.
GOOD, BECAUSE I DON'T THINK YOU'R GOING TO LIKE WHA ASKED OF YOU.

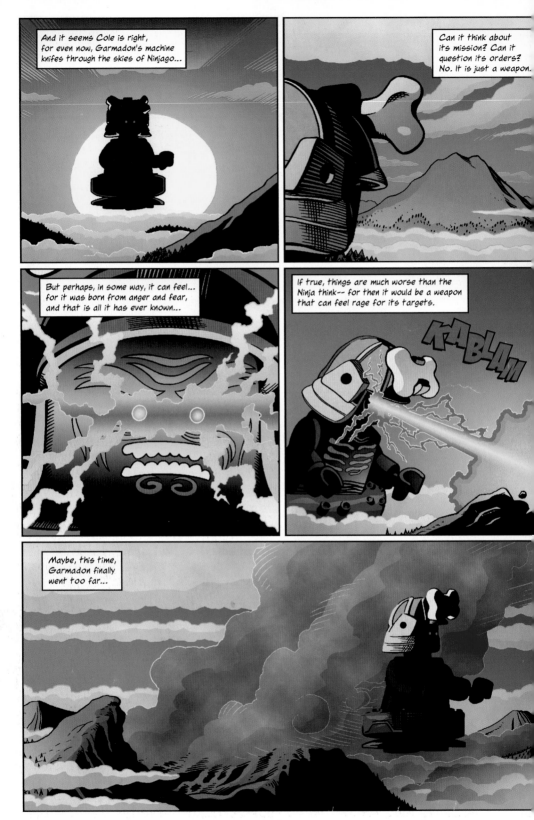

And it seems Cole is right, for even now, Garmadon's machine knifes through the skies of Ninjago...

Can it think about its mission? Can it question its orders? No. It is just a weapon.

But perhaps, in some way, it can feel... for it was born from anger and fear, and that is all it has ever known...

If true, things are much worse than the Ninja think-- for then it would be a weapon that can feel rage for its targets.

KABLAM

Maybe, this time, Garmadon finally went too far...

The next morning, Garmadon leads the Ninja to a strange site: a tar pit in the center of the jungle.

WELL, I HAVEN'T SEEN ANYTHING LIKE THIS BEFORE.

INDEED. IT CANNOT BE A NATURAL FEATURE OF THIS AREA.

IT'S NOT. SAMUKAI AND I CREATED IT TO HIDE THE FINAL PIECE.

SO WE GO DOWN THERE AND GET IT.

YOU WOULDN'T LAST A MINUTE, KAI. THIS STUFF IS BOILING HOT.

THE FOURTH PIECE WON'T EMERGE UNTIL THE REST OF THE MACHINE GETS HERE.

WHEN IT DOES, ZANE AND I WILL GO TO WORK-- THE REST OF YOU WILL BACK US UP.

WHY LEAVE THE OTHERS BEHIND?

ZANE IS THE ONLY ONE WHO CAN DO HIS PART OF THIS JOB. IT'S ALL PART OF THE PLAN.

SO ALL WE GET TO DO IS WATCH?

SO IT'S OUR EASIEST MISSION, OR OUR LAST, TAKE YOUR PICK.

WATCH AND HOPE... WHILE MY DAD IS RISKING HIS LIFE SO WE CAN HANG ONTO OURS.

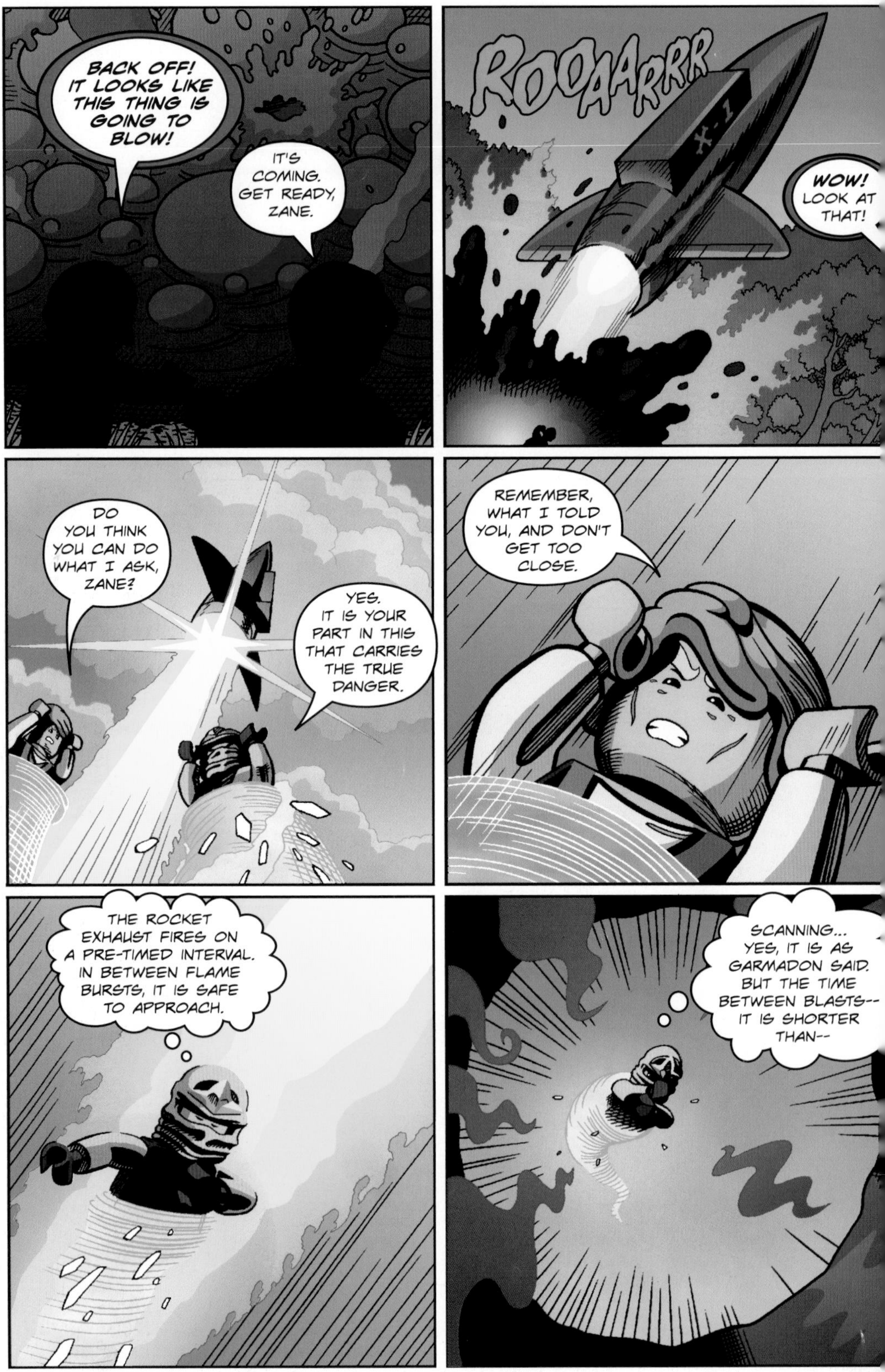
BACK OFF! IT LOOKS LIKE THIS THING IS GOING TO BLOW!
IT'S COMING. GET READY, ZANE.
ROOAARRR
X-1
WOW! LOOK AT THAT!
DO YOU THINK YOU CAN DO WHAT I ASK, ZANE?
YES. IT IS YOUR PART IN THIS THAT CARRIES THE TRUE DANGER.
REMEMBER, WHAT I TOLD YOU, AND DON'T GET TOO CLOSE.
THE ROCKET EXHAUST FIRES ON A PRE-TIMED INTERVAL. IN BETWEEN FLAME BURSTS, IT IS SAFE TO APPROACH.
SCANNING... YES, IT IS AS GARMADON SAID. BUT THE TIME BETWEEN BLASTS-- IT IS SHORTER THAN--

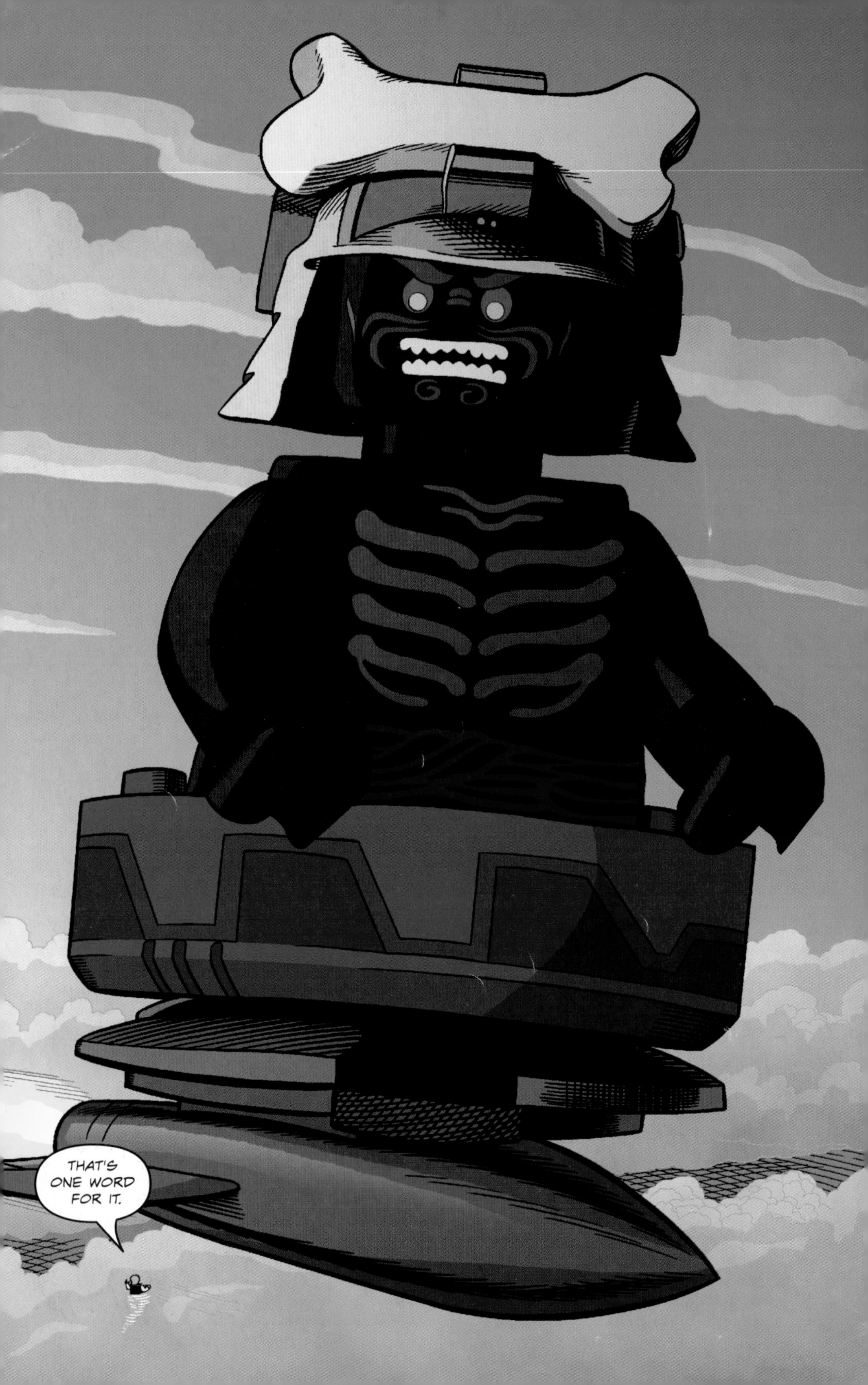
THAT'S ONE WORD FOR IT.

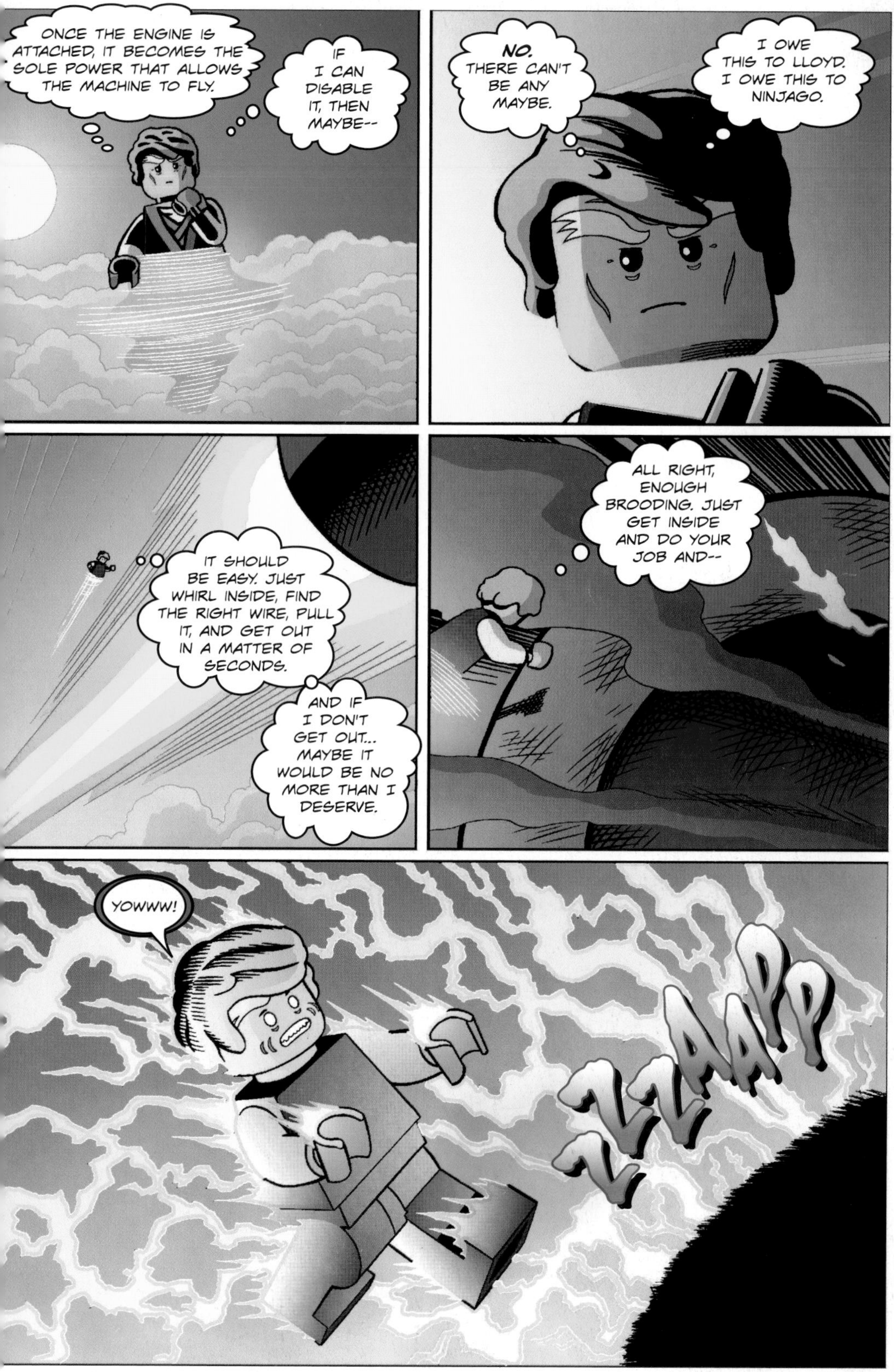
ONCE THE ENGINE IS ATTACHED, IT BECOMES THE SOLE POWER THAT ALLOWS THE MACHINE TO FLY.
IF I CAN DISABLE IT, THEN MAYBE--
NO. THERE CAN'T BE ANY MAYBE.
I OWE THIS TO LLOYD. I OWE THIS TO NINJAGO.
IT SHOULD BE EASY. JUST WHIRL INSIDE, FIND THE RIGHT WIRE, PULL IT, AND GET OUT IN A MATTER OF SECONDS.
AND IF I DON'T GET OUT... MAYBE IT WOULD BE NO MORE THAN I DESERVE.
ALL RIGHT, ENOUGH BROODING. JUST GET INSIDE AND DO YOUR JOB AND--
YOWWW!
ZZZAPP

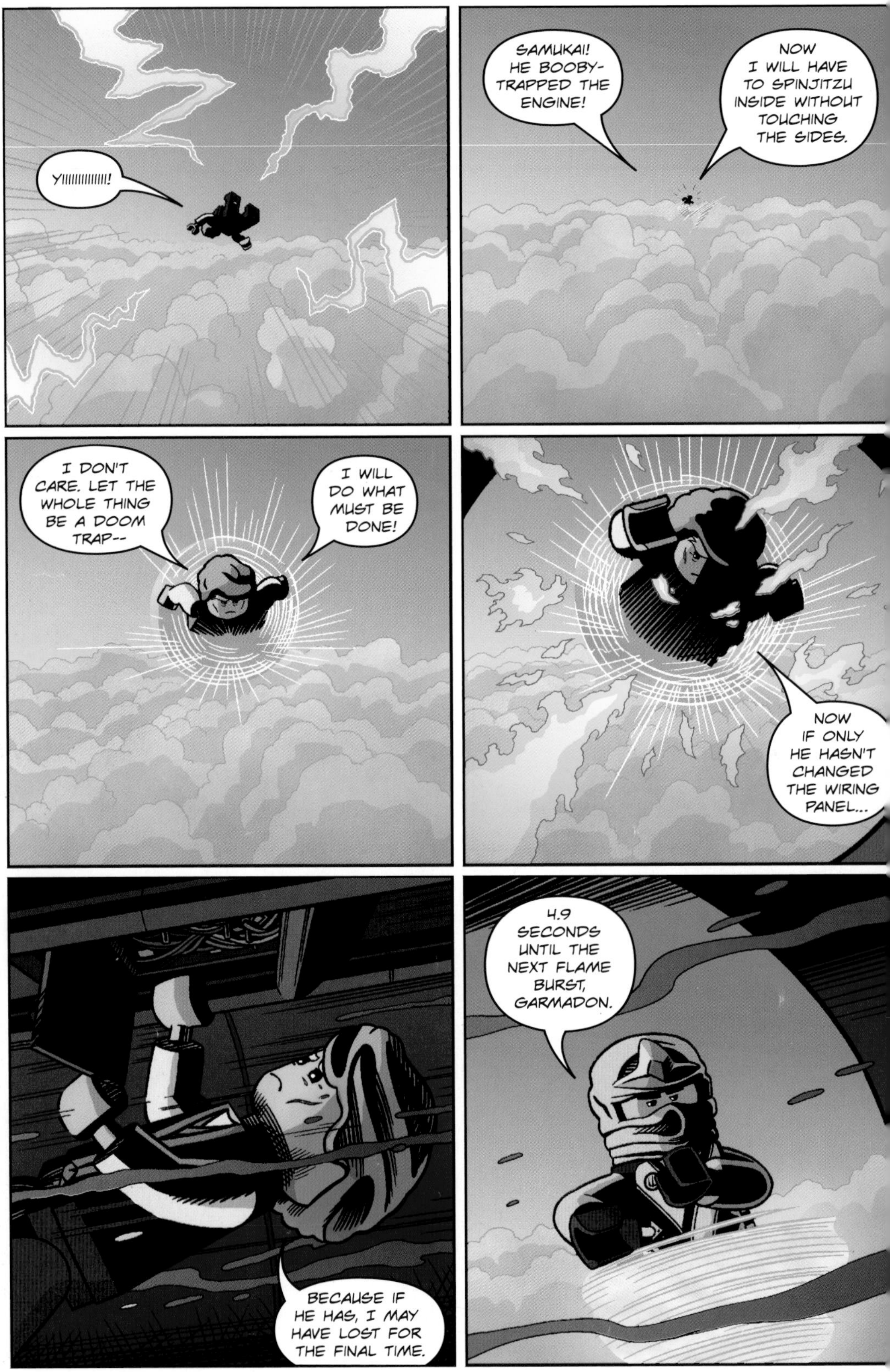
YIIIIIIIIIIII!
SAMUKAI! HE BOOBY-TRAPPED THE ENGINE!
NOW I WILL HAVE TO SPINJITZU INSIDE WITHOUT TOUCHING THE SIDES.
I DON'T CARE. LET THE WHOLE THING BE A DOOM TRAP--
I WILL DO WHAT MUST BE DONE!
NOW IF ONLY HE HASN'T CHANGED THE WIRING PANEL...
BECAUSE IF HE HAS, I MAY HAVE LOST FOR THE FINAL TIME.
4.9 SECONDS UNTIL THE NEXT FLAME BURST, GARMADON.

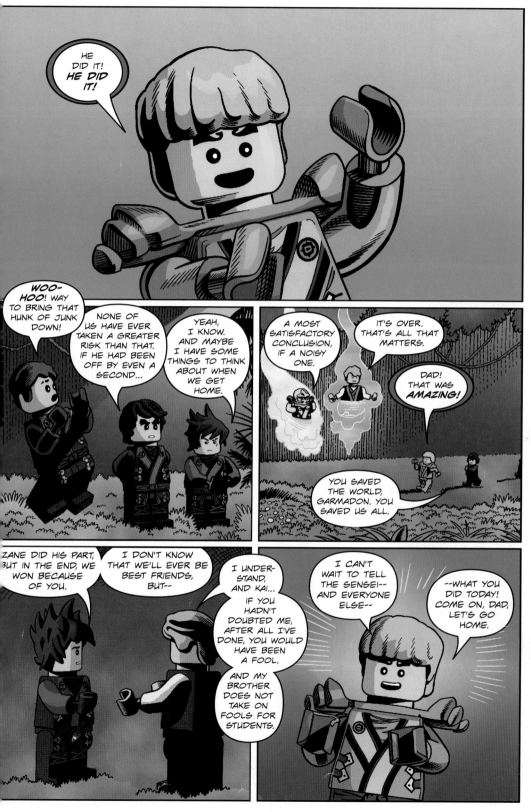

WATCH OUT FOR PAPERCUTZ™

Welcome to the enlightening, engaging, and inevitably entrapping eighth LEGO® NINJAGO graphic novel from Papercutz, the deconstructed comics company dedicated to publishing great graphic novels for all ages! I'm your Green (Ninja) Tea-sipping Editor-in-Chief, Jim Salicrup just back from the Biggest Comicbook Show on Earth! Of course I'm talking about the 2013 Comic-Con International.

Like last year, we were honored again when the Hageman Brothers, the brilliant writers of the animated LEGO Ninjago Cartoon Network TV series, stopped by the Papercutz booth to pick up the new LEGO Ninjago poster by Jolyon Yates. They both shared a few exciting secrets about the future of LEGO Ninjago, but since we're sworn to secrecy we can't tell you anything except the best is yet to come for our favorite masters of Spinjitzu!

Of course, Jolyon Yates was also at the Papercutz booth (along with our Marketing Director Jesse Post, Production Coordinator Beth Scorzato, and Publisher Terry Nantier) signing posters, and on Sunday, drawing lots of free sketches of Jay, Cole, Zane, and Kai. Seeing all the enthusiastic LEGO NINJAGO fans was great fun and it re-energized us all. We're working harder than ever to make the upcoming LEGO NINJAGO graphic novels better than anything you've seen so far! For example, we've got a bonus Lloyd story planned for LEGO NINJAGO #9! That should be available around the same time as The LEGO Movie is released—which in addition to appearances by Batman, Superman, Wonder Woman, a Teenage Mutant Ninja Turtle (Leonardo), and others, also features the Green Ninja!

So, until next time, keep spinnin'! Ninja-GO!

Jim

Jim with Kevin and Dan Hageman.
Or is it Dan and Kevin?

Jolyon Yates drawing crowds and ninja at the Papercutz booth.

STAY IN TOUCH!

EMAIL: salicrup@papercutz.com
WEB: papercutz.com
TWITTER: @papercutzgn
FACEBOOK: PAPERCUTZGRAPHICNOVELS
SNAIL MAIL: Papercutz, 160 Broadway, Suite 700, East Wing, New York, NY 10038

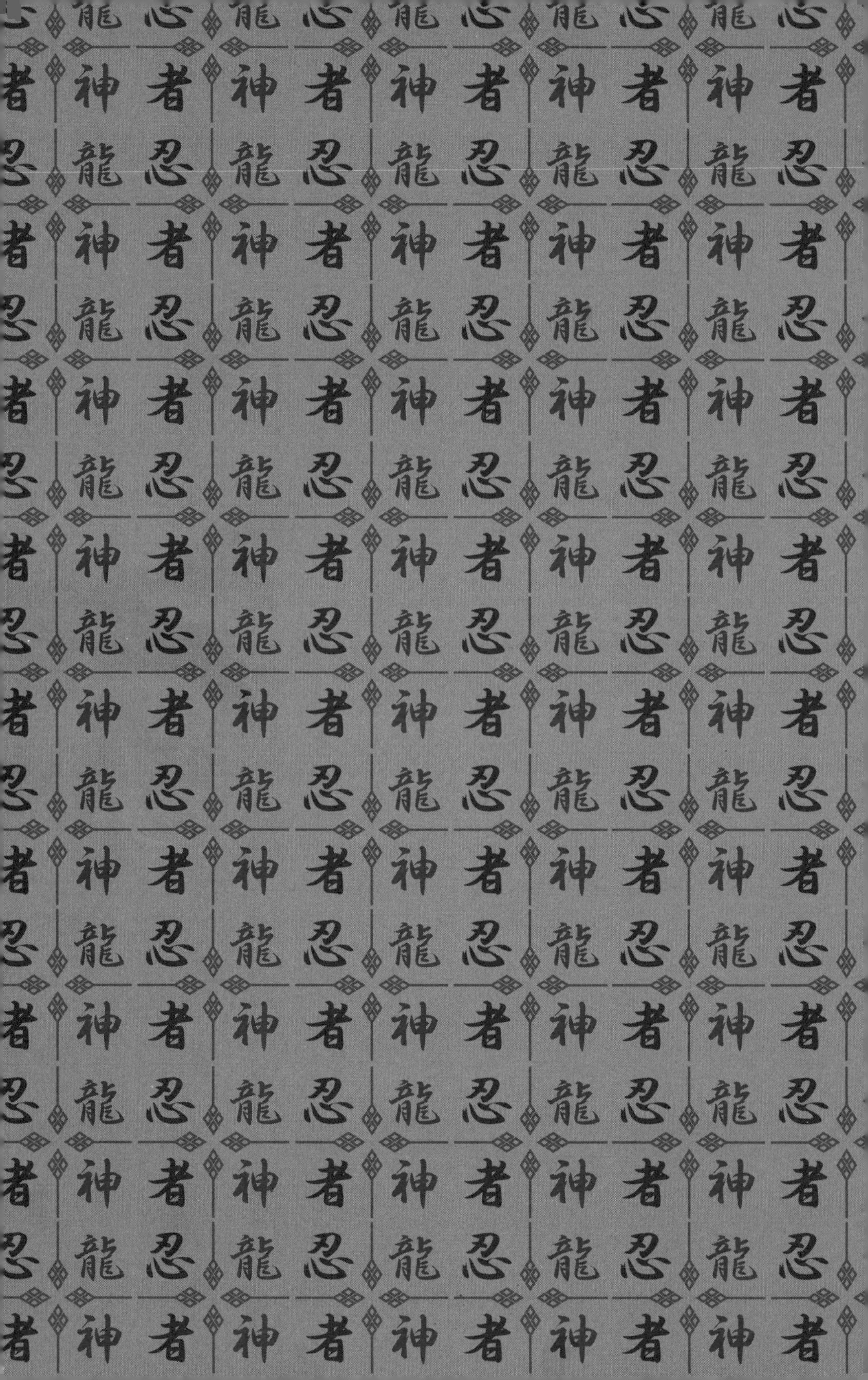
忍者
神龍